the way things always happen here

for my parents, Hobert and Nancy Stewart

and in remembrance of

Jim Whitehead,

Scott Christianson,

and Brian Wilkie

contents

acknowledgments

The author wishes to thank the following readers for their help on some or all of these stories: Ed Davis, Randolph Thomas, Jay Prefontaine, John Hennessy, Michael Catherwood, Michael Garriga, Eric Schmitt, and Lisa Balonis.

Thanks to Skip Hays, Bill Harrison, Joanne Meschery, and everyone else in the University of Arkansas' Programs in Creative Writing, the hardest-working and hardest-living MFA program in all of academia!

Thanks to the West Virginia and Louisiana state arts commissions for their financial support.

Thanks to The Chimes.

Thanks to Grace Edwards, Tim Poland, Moira Baker, and all the other folks at Radford University for taking a big chance on a B student.

And, finally, thanks to Pat Conner, Sara Pritchard, Stacey Elza, Than Saffel, and everyone else at West Virginia University Press for their support and hard work.

one mississippi

My buddy Eddie and I were at the Oak County Airport, but we were supposed to be drinking, riding some back road. That morning, I'd registered for the draft, stopped by the liquor store (back then you only had to be eighteen to buy booze), and picked up Eddie. When he said to go to the airport, I had a hunch about what he was up to, but I asked why anyway.

"I figure I got one last shot to help you make your old man shut up about his Air Force story," Eddie said.

When my old man was in boot camp, between Korea and Vietnam, he had to cut the barracks' lawn with a pair of grade-school scissors because he puked at the top of a fifty-foot high-diving platform, during the high-dive drills, right into the pool. The drill sergeant pushed Dad off, and Dad belly-flopped puke and pool water everywhere. That was his war story, and he told it to me with regret and malice. He also told it as if I would've reacted worse.

I'd inherited my old man's fear of heights. Eddie had been skydiving since he was fourteen, and every so often he took it upon himself to help me get over my phobia by trying it. He was the kind of guy who'd throw his kid in the river to teach him to swim. Although the thought of skydiving scared me, part of me wanted to jump because of my old man's story, but the rest of me wanted to because of something else he'd said: that I was taking the easy way through life—college. Both, good reasons to jump, but would they be enough when the time came? If not, the booze would surely help push me over the edge.

Eddie knew a pilot, Barry, for InCor Coal Company, who also taught skydiving. We found him in one of the hangars, washing down a single-engine plane. When Eddie told him we needed a couple of chutes, Barry said he couldn't take us up.

I was relieved.

"We don't need no plane," Eddie said.

Barry and I stared at him.

"College Boy here needs to get over his fear of heights," Eddie said. "'Less he wants to go off to college knowing they's one thing he can't do that I can."

I knew Eddie was trying to get a rise out of me. He was headed to Summit State, the local commuter college, to major in electrical engineering. Because of my good grades and test scores, I'd earned a free ride to any state college or university. I chose Shepherd College, five hours away in the eastern panhandle—as far away from Triple Oaks as possible, but still in West Virginia.

Barry said he didn't want to know anything about it, but he let us borrow two parachutes. Eddie assured him nothing would go wrong, and we stuffed the chutes in the front of my VW Beetle. I didn't know what Eddie had in mind. It worried me, and what little nerve I'd mustered was waning, booze or no booze. "Head for the interstate, Lawson," Eddie said as we pulled away from the airport.

"Where're we going?" I asked.

"Just drive. You'll find out when we get there." Then he started laughing.

"What's so funny?" I said, thinking he was laughing at me for some reason.

"My old man," he said. "He damn sure looked funny in that picture, drinking that fifth. He ever says anything about me drinking, I'll shove that picture right in his goddamn Sunday-school-teaching face."

I glanced at him. "Hell, Eddie, that was a long time ago. His first time away from home probably." He stared straight ahead. Last weekend, his old man had caught us drunk, celebrating my eighteenth birthday. I'd brought Eddie home, and his dad was waiting for us on the porch. "Oh, shit," Eddie said as he pushed from the car. I should've taken off, but I wanted to see what would happen. I knew Eddie—who wouldn't turn eighteen until August—and his old man didn't get along well, and maybe I have a slight morbid curiosity. Maybe this was also why I let Eddie direct me to wherever we were going. When Eddie reached his porch, his dad stood and got in his face, as though sniffing Eddie's breath. Then he started motioning for me. I wanted to gun it, but I knew better. Afraid he'd call my old man, I turned off the ignition and trudged toward them.

After taking us inside, he made us sit at each end of the couch. From a bookshelf, he pulled what looked like a yearbook from the end of a line of *Reader's Digest* condensed books and sat between us. He opened the book, an Air Force yearbook from 1956, to a dog-eared page and pointed to a young, plump-faced man with a crew cut and a cleft chin. His eyes reflected the flashbulb like fine gems. His teeth, in a wide smile, were all white and even. His right hand gripped a liquor bottle.

"That was me," he said. "'Bout y'all's age. Within a year, I was an alcoholic, if I wasn't already in this picture. Wrecked a couple of jeeps, drunk, and got dishonorably discharged."

I looked at him. His face was still plump, but it was lined with age—at the corners of his eyes, around his nose, across his forehead. A graying beard that looked as rough as steel wool covered most of his chin, jowls, and neck. He was now bald on top, the overhead light glaring on the shiny skin there, and his eyes were as gray as tweed.

"I ain't telling y'all this to preach no morals or nothing," he said, "but they ain't no good can come from drinking."

We sat there silently.

"I could get you arrested for him being drunk," he said to me.

"Yessir," I said.

"I ain't though," he said. "But don't come around him no more. Next time, you won't be so lucky."

"I won't, sir." I glanced at Eddie, but he wouldn't look at me. Then I left.

That was Eddie's old man's war story. I guess I should've felt bad for him, but I was pissed that he forbade me to come around, not that I was all that close to Eddie. I figured Eddie would be here forever—there are sixty thousand Eddies stuck in Oak County, and they don't even know they're stuck. It's as if East River Mountain, which forms the border between West Virginia and Virginia to the south, acts as a big dam, hiding the world from them. And these people are fish in this dead-end lake. They swim to the dam, only to return to their familiar confines, unconscious of the barrier. A few somehow trickle through the tunnel into Bland County and on into North Carolina, but not many.

Though I felt imprisoned there, shackled to Oak County by family, by the way your hometown can define you, I'd been telling myself for a long time that I was better than all of them. I'd get out. But you still need someone to run around with. For me, that someone was Eddie. Now, because of our run-in with his old man, the stakes had been raised.

When Eddie said to take US 19 at Beckley, I understood his plan. I'd seen people jump from the New River Gorge Bridge on Bridge Day—every October there were broken limbs, sprains, concussions. Occasionally, someone died. "The bridge?" I asked, but I knew the answer.

He grinned and played air guitar to Alice Cooper's "I'm Eighteen."

We drove down into New River Gorge, parked, drank, and listened to the whine of tires on the bridge above us. The hot evening air was thick with pollen and dandelion seedlings and humidity and the sounds of traffic and birds and the river gurgling past. The leaves on the trees drooped lifelessly, as if they'd been dipped in clear syrup. Soon, a bunch of rafters from Thurmond beached across the river from us and stormed onto waiting rafting-company buses and left.

Listening to the vehicles on the bridge, I was trying to imagine what jumping from it would be like. I couldn't picture it, couldn't conjure up any sensations other than terror. But Eddie seemed confident, so I tried to appear at ease.

"I done signed up," Eddie finally said after the rafters were gone. He'd been quiet for a while.

"For what?"

"The army."

I looked at him. "What about college?"

"I made a goddamn eleven on my ACT." He drank from the fifth, swallowed hard. "I can't get in no college."

"Hell, Eddie, anyone can get in Summit State," I said, but instantly wished I could take it back. Summit State had open admissions. People joked that their motto was "Pay your fee, get your degree."

"Not with no goddamn eleven," he said after another pull.

"Study for the test. Take it again."

"Ain't gonna do no good, man," he said. "I took the diagnostic test down at the recruiter's office. You know what I'm qualified to do with the score I made?"

"What?"

"Be a M.P."

"What's wrong with an M.P.?"

"Only thing lower is K.P." He finished off the Jack, climbed from the car, and exploded the bottle against a "No Dumping" sign in front of us. "I can do goddamn K.P. at Hardee's," he said to the river. Then he turned and looked at me. "But in the army, if I work my ass off, I might could become a paratrooper."

"Why didn't you tell me?"

"Had to make sure I was in first."

I climbed out of the car and looked up into the sky. The walls of the gorge were steep, the horizon straight up. I wondered if this was why most people around here could only understand the future as tomorrow. In these hollows, you can't see much farther than you can piss. Everything's immediate, even foresight.

"You should try seeing this place from the sky," Eddie said, as if reading my mind. "The first time I jumped from an airplane, I saw the mountains trail off flat. They give out and weren't nothing. They's things out there, man." I studied him a moment. He stared at the bridge as if it were the neighborhood bully and Eddie wasn't going to take any more. I grew a little more confident in him. "Eight-hundred and seventy-six feet to the river," Eddie said. "The highest bridge east of the Mississippi."

"You jumped from it already?" I was hoping, needing something to give me even more confidence.

"Nope, but I been studying on it."

"Why don't we wait till Bridge Day, when we can do it legally?"

"You'll be in the goddamn Thumb by then."

The "Thumb" is the eastern panhandle. You can make a replica of the state of West Virginia with your right hand simply by giving the finger while sticking your thumb out. We lived down near the wrist. The bridge crossed the life line.

"Cops'll nab us up there before we even make it to the middle," I said.

"We're gonna do it in the dark."

"In the dark?"

"It's all timing," he said. "You count to three, then toss the pilot chute, and I don't care if the sky's blue, black, or silver or five shades of green with pink polka dots, you ain't gonna fall no faster or no slower. The bottom is still eight-hundred and seventy-six feet down."

I looked up again. The bridge looked thin as a ruler it was so high. I tried to imagine not seeing it against a night sky, just hearing the whine of those radial tires, watching the faint glow of headlights bleed over the edge of the concrete railing. Would the drop be as frightening if you couldn't see the bottom?

Eddie unpacked and repacked the chutes, checked the pilot chutes, and then stuffed our headgear in the packs.

An hour later, the shadow of the ridge behind us had blanketed the gorge, bringing on the night. We'd made a good-sized dent in a fifth of vodka. Lightning bugs rose from the weeds and bushes. The gorge sang with crickets, cicadas, doves, frogs, and whippoorwills.

"Hear that whippoorwill?" Eddie said. "Means somebody's gonna die."

I glanced at him. "Shut the hell up."

Eddie laughed, gave me a good-natured punch in the arm. "Let's head up," he said. "Traffic'll thin out after a while. We'll look like a couple of hitchers walking across."

We strapped the chutes on and followed an overgrown logging road that zigzagged its way up to the visitors center at the top. When we crested the ridge, we stayed in the woods for a while, sipping vodka and waiting for full darkness. There was no moon. Despite the booze, staring at the bridge was having a sobering effect on me. From the woods, we could see only about one-quarter of the way down into the gorge, but I knew what I didn't see was still there—that long drop to the bottom—despite the trees in the foreground, the musical darkness below.

"I might ask Rhonda Compton to marry me," Eddie said and passed the bottle to me.

Another unexpected revelation, but the information in this one was even more surprising than in the first. "Rhonda Compton?" I knew he'd been seeing her, but I'd thought only for sex, just like the other several dozen guys she'd been with. Marrying her was a bad idea. "Hell, Eddie, she's screwed everybody in Triple Oaks." In the back of my mind, I was hoping he'd get mad at me and the jump would be off.

He looked at me and grinned. "Hell, Triple Oaks ain't no big town." I watched him a moment longer and then shook my head and laughed. I took another pull and handed him the bottle. His disclosures made me feel a little closer to him, but they also made me feel like a stranger.

Then he told me how to jump: you fall sixteen feet the first second, doubling the distance every second after that; hold the pilot chute in your hand, go "one-Mississippi, two-Mississippi, three-Mississippi," let go, and out comes the main chute; guide yourself with the handles; tug left to go left, right to go right, but do whatever you have to do to miss the water; you can just walk right onto the ground. The whole thing takes about ten seconds.

I looked at the bridge, which is nearly two-thirds of a mile long. When we started across, it seemed to stretch all the way back to Triple Oaks, about eighty miles south. The wind howled across the span, and you could feel the bridge move, especially when the tractor trailers crossed. The booze had made the queasiness in my stomach worse. I'd vowed to myself not to puke, though, so I never looked down. The weight of my parachute felt as though it pushed my steps a few extra millimeters into the concrete decking, and those brief moments of rootedness made me thankful.

Near the center, we slowed our pace, waiting for a lone set of headlights to zip past. Only a tractor trailer, heading south and yet to reach the bridge, was coming in the other direction. The car passed, a blurred moon of a face watching us from the passenger window. Eddie put on his headgear and dug mine from my pack, placed it on my head and cinched the strap snugly under my chin. I felt awkward, like a kid, my old man trying to dress me in the rough way that men do those kinds of things because something deep down makes them feel uncomfortable doing them—changing diapers, or the urine bag of an invalid father. My grandfather had survived war, earned a medal and then returned home, to West Virginia, to be slowly killed by the mines. Black lung and arthritis. In our back bedroom, my old man tended to him the last ten years of his life, including the first five of my life. Then came my mother's cancer.

"Let's go," Eddie said. He climbed over the barrier and stood on the eight-inch-wide overhang. I hesitated a moment, took a deep breath, and climbed over with him. I dug my heels into the overhang, bracing my ass against the barrier but still not looking down. "Wind's in our face. You gotta jump out so you don't get blown into the structure."

The truck rumbled past, vibrating the bridge, and I grasped the top of the cool concrete barrier, afraid of getting shaken off. "Don't worry," Eddie said. "The bridge is supposed to move like that." I'd convinced myself to trust his parachute knowledge, but did he know as much about bridges?

He took the last swig of vodka and tossed the bottle straight ahead. We never heard it hit bottom.

"Who's going first?" he asked.

"Go."

Off he went, yelling. His scream trailed off, and I finally looked down. It was pitch dark, except for the whitecaps of the river upstream. Then Eddie's chute exploded open like the flash of a camera. He started angling in the direction of my car. From the south, to my right, traffic drew nearer. At least a dozen cars were coming. Several more rounded the turn to the north, also headed toward me. I looked down again. Eddie's chute was there a moment longer and then was sucked back into the darkness. For all I knew he could've been dead down there.

I was alone up here. There were no more instructions, no pep talks. Just me and the wind and lines of cars coming in both directions. I was about to chicken out and had almost decided to walk off the bridge and follow that fire road back down. My excuse would be I was worried about him, and if I got hurt too, who'd help us? He'd know better. And somehow my old man would find out.

I scanned the irregular horizon, which was just a shade darker than the sky. Eddie had seen it from thousands of feet above and sensed real freedom. I wanted to know it too.

His instructions came back to me. I ran the details of them, the confidence with which he'd told them, through my mind. Closing my eyes, I held my breath and jumped, but I didn't yell. The pilot chute clenched in my right fist, I counted to three-Mississippi so quickly I know I skipped syllables. Then I tossed the pilot chute from my hand as if rolling dice.

The chute yanked me up, snapping me out of my free fall, which jarred the air from my lungs and seemed to jerk all of my bones into my feet. My legs felt like empty socks with bowling balls in the toes. The harness tightened around my chest as I slowed down. Trying to breathe, I opened my eyes and grabbed the guide handles, settling into the glide. I felt detached from this place, free, safe. I could float down like this forever—weightless, rootless. I thought about Shepherd—far from here, but still here. It wasn't the answer. I felt myself grow heavier with something cold and thick and black. The gorge was pulling me back down, and gravity can show you some hard realities.

I had to get ready to land because the land was waiting to crush me with the weight of myself, which had trickled back into place. I took a slow breath. The vague outlines of trees on the canyon sides composed themselves out of the darkness. Looking up, I could see only the chute; looking down, I could begin to make out the bottom. The whitecaps in the river came into focus, and then the beach. I was centered over the water. Eight hundred and seventy-six feet suddenly seemed no thicker than the skin of a bubble.

"Steer to your right," Eddie was yelling, semaphoring from the river's edge. I pulled down on the right handle. The chute tilted hard and spun in a semicircle. The alcohol wheeled in my stomach, and I held my breath again. My guts and throat burned.

"Not so hard," Eddie yelled. I eased off and exhaled and thought about broken legs, concussions, drowning. The river was right under me. I started working my legs as though pedaling a bicycle. My right foot stomped into the water and hit the bottom. I splashed forward onto my left foot, my right. I tripped and the momentum from the jump slammed me face-first into the water. Its warm current washed over me and started tugging my chute, which had settled in the water behind me. I thought I might get swept away, down to the confluence with the Gauley, the Kanawha, to the Ohio, the Mississippi. For a moment it was a relaxing feeling.

But Eddie was there, lifting me out, unhooking the chute.

I gained my footing on the bottom and stood, my shoes settling into the river gravel. Water rained from my clothes. I was waist-deep, soaked, scared, and short of breath, but I felt an exciting buzz. Eddie hugged me and I hugged him back. "Hell yeah!" he yelled and looked up at the bridge. "We beat the hell out of that son of a bitch!"

"Yeah," I said, shivering from the water, the jump.

"How'd it feel?" he asked, still supporting me as if I might fall.

I glanced at him, gave him a quick grin. He had the look of someone who'd just shown you a guarded secret but one that gave him a lot of pride. He laughed as I pulled away. Then we started hauling in the chute.

At home, Dad was sitting on the couch, in the dim glow of a table lamp. "Eddie's daddy called," he said. "Said Eddie was drunk. Said you give it to him."

Damp and cold, I stood there, unafraid. He looked at me, saw my wet clothes. "The hell you get all wet?"

I glanced down at myself and then back at him. The story of my jump began to form itself in my mouth. I was ready to tell him what I'd done, to humiliate him, but in the low light of the living room, he appeared ashamed of me. I blinked the story from my mind. "We were having some fun at New River," I said. "Things got out of hand."

"You know how many people drown in that river? And you with your clothes on," he said. "Ain't you got no better sense than that?"

Feeling colder, I crossed my arms over my chest and tried not to shiver.

"I think I talked him out of pressing any charges," Dad said. "Told him it won't happen anymore. You was leaving soon."

I nodded at him and started upstairs but stopped when he spoke again. "If your mother was still here, you would of killed her acting like this, then just up and leaving it all behind. You can't just wipe the slate clean, boy."

I stood there, faced away from him, and closed my eyes.

"You can't just leave."

His words dripped from my back, and the silence sagged between us. I kept my eyes closed and took myself back to the gorge. I was standing in that swift water again, leaning against the current. River gravel sluiced from under my shoes.

the way things always happen here

The man from the bank told Mr. Sommers the cops had the car hosed out, but everything would have to be replaced, foam and all, to get rid of the stains and the smell. The bank wanted to resell it. We all peered inside. On the gray carpet and front and back seats were bloodstains the color of iodine. The car smelled like soured hamburger packaging and soap. Mr. Sommers jotted down some numbers on an estimate pad. "I'll reorder the carpet and the seat foam," he told the man from the bank, "but we'll have to make the seat covers and recover the head liner and sun visors."

"Whatever you gotta do," the man said. "The key's in it." He gave Mr. Sommers a business card and left with the driver.

The best friend of my girlfriend, Colleen, was killed in the Cutlass. The girl's name was Elizabeth. She was eighteen. Her twenty-five-year-old boyfriend took her up on Oak Mountain above Summit and put a bullet in her temple because she was leaving him for college at WVU. Then he shot himself. Some lost traveler wanting directions found them.

I looked at the car. The sun glinted off its clean chrome trim, the grill, the windshield. It looked almost new. I figured there were at least three years' worth of payments owed on it. It was last year's model.

"I'd hate to be the one that buys it next," Mr. Sommers said.

"Colleen's future college roommate died in there," I said.

"I heard about that. Colleen all right?"

"Numb," I said. "Who wouldn't be?"

"Too bad the sonofabitch didn't start with hisself," he said and nodded at the car. "Well, better pull it on inside. You might wanna lay a towel or something over the seat first."

I got a shop towel from inside, took a deep breath, and laid the towel on the seat and jumped inside. The car started on the first try. In the shop, I cranked down all the windows, hopped out, and breathed. I watched the car a moment. The sound of a pistol in there must have been deafening. And he must have had blood all over himself, moist and warm. There's no turning back then. I wondered if he heard that last shot.

That evening, I drove straight home from work and showered for about thirty minutes. I didn't have to get back in the car that afternoon, but the few seconds I was in there seemed to cling to me the rest of the day.

I twisted up three or four joints and stuck them in the pocket of my T-shirt. Colleen and I'd planned to go out later, but I decided to hold off telling her about the car. I didn't know how she'd react, whether she'd want to see it right away, whether she'd want me to quit work because of it. How would she act if she knew I'd sat on those stains?

After Elizabeth's funeral two days earlier, Colleen stopped by the shop. She said she was almost afraid to go to WVU now, alone. Like an idiot, I told her she was better off getting away from it all, but I found hope in what she'd said, hope that she might stay here.

They'd been friends since meeting in All-County Choir during junior high. They were both honor students, but at different high schools: Colleen at Carthage, Elizabeth at Summit. When they got to

WVU together, Colleen said, they were planning to skip classes, crash parties, stay high, laugh at the sorority girls, but still make good grades. I planned to visit every weekend. I'd decided to take a class at nearby Oak College, even after being out of high school two years and working for Mr. Sommers even longer. I wanted to try to keep something in common between Colleen and me.

"Why don't you move with me?" she asked.

I told her I couldn't leave my job, but I smiled at her and said, "You'll see plenty of me."

"You promise?"

I held her. "It'll be like you never left."

Colleen was sitting on her front-porch steps when I pulled up. As soon as she saw me, she ran toward me. Her hair was tied in a ponytail, and she wore cut-off blue-jean shorts and a Patti Smith T-shirt. "How was work?" she asked when she climbed in.

I turned down Springsteen's *The River* on the cassette player. "Pretty much the same."

"Well, the RA at the honors dorm called today. She told me I could room alone if I want, because of what happened to Elizabeth."

"Don't you get all A's in college if your roommate dies?"

She glared at me. "I wouldn't use Elizabeth's death to make A's."

"Sorry," I said. "That's just what I've always heard."

"My dad said that's just a myth." Her dad was a professor at Oak. She'd grown up around more books than I'd ever seen, except for the library. My old man hated her and her family. That was one of the first things that attracted me to her. She'd made me a better student when I was in school and had encouraged me to go to Oak when I graduated two years ago. I just wanted to get out of the house then, so I got a job instead. Now I wished I'd listened to her.

I took a joint from my pocket and handed it to her. We headed down Pumphouse Road and then turned onto a dirt road. When we reached the top of the hill at Pisgah Road, the sun had disappeared. Dusk had turned the mountains to a bruise color. I could see red lights flashing atop the Towers dorms at Oak College to my right. Straight ahead, north, ten or fifteen miles distant, the tiny headlights and taillights of cars and trucks ascended and descended the interstate. I pulled over at a wide spot, watching the strip of highway where Colleen would be driving in a week, headed for Morgantown. I thought about coming to this spot when she left, and I'd watch that section of I-77 for her to pass by. Maybe I'd bring binoculars.

"When you leave, go at night," I said.

"Why?"

"See the road?" I pointed to where I-77 met the sky.

She looked at the road and nodded.

"When you get to that spot, shut off your lights."

"And drive in the dark?"

I nodded.

"A little dangerous, don't you think?"

"It's straight. Follow the taillights ahead of you. I'll be able to see you for the last possible second."

She smiled at me. "That's nice, Allen."

For a few moments we sat there silently, smoking and drinking and watching the road. As badly as I wanted to tell her about the car, I couldn't. She might think I was using it to make her stay, and I was sure she'd be right.

After we'd shared all of the pot and warm beer, we automatically climbed in back of the van and undressed in the darkness, as though it were the next logical step on a night like this. It was the first sex we'd had since Elizabeth's death. I don't know why, but I'd been almost afraid to touch Colleen.

The Cutlass had to be stripped the next day. The only employee at the shop who wasn't one of Mr. Sommers's relatives, I was the logical choice for the job. I got all the shit jobs. I began by unbolting the front bench-seat. After Mr. Sommers helped me carry it from the car to a worktable, I started picking up crap that the cops had left under the seat. They weren't thorough in their cleaning. Among the fast-food garbage and condom wrappers was a window scraper, a half-empty pint of Canadian Mist, $1.27 in change (one of the fringe benefits of the upholstery business), a tube of lipstick, beer bottle caps, a Polaroid of Elizabeth (well-tanned in a white bikini), and a WVU catalogue not too damaged by the hosing.

I opened the catalogue to place the Polaroid inside and saw a picture of three frat boys walking down a sidewalk, smiling. Pistols had been drawn in ink, and they pointed at each boy's temple. I turned a few more pages and saw a guy in a study lounge with a gun at his head. I flipped through the whole catalogue. Every picture of a male had an inked-in pistol aimed at his head, even a picture of a section of crowd at a WVU football game.

The guy was insane, but you wouldn't have known it from meeting him. I'd been around him once, on a double date with Colleen and Elizabeth. He was stocky, clean-cut, and quiet, and he worked at a machine shop. He didn't talk unless asked a question. His ears and neck flushed whenever Colleen and Elizabeth mentioned WVU. Later, Colleen had told me Elizabeth's boyfriend made her nervous. "He's so quiet," she said. "Not shy quiet or polite quiet. Weird quiet, like he's always up to something."

I put his money in my pocket and took the Canadian Mist, the picture, and the book to my van.

I dismantled the seats and pulled the velour covers off, stiff with dried blood. The foam, too, was stained, so I threw everything but the metal seat frames into the trash. I took out the rear seat and removed the safety belts, step moldings, carpet trim. I ripped out the carpet and felt padding and wrestled them into the trash, too.

I twisted the door-lock knobs off. Using a Phillips screwdriver, I removed the armrests from the doors and popped off the panels. Blood had leaked between the window and the rubber gasket, hardening into puddles along the inside of the door frame. I used a toilet-bowl brush and undiluted disinfectant cleaner to scrub in there and to scrub the dashboard, the exposed metal, the steering wheel and column, and the grooves around the glove box, radio, gauges, and heater and air-conditioning controls.

After taking down the sun visors, aluminum door and window trim, dome light, and coat-hanger hooks, I removed the headliner and carried it to a worktable. The cops hadn't cleaned the headliner off well, either. Traces of Elizabeth and her boyfriend were flecked all over it—bits of skin, clumps of dried blood, fragments of skull, and matted hanks of hair. The foam-backed cloth, which was glued to a pressboard mold that fit the underside of the car's top, had to be stripped off. I peeled away enough cloth from the corner to get a fingerhold and pulled the cloth with my left hand and scraped with my right, using a putty knife. It was like skinning an animal. Once the material was off the mold, I rolled it up, wrapped it with masking tape, and chucked it in the trash with the rest.

It should've been a full day's job, but I finished by three that afternoon and told Mr. Sommers I needed to take the rest of the day off. He agreed.

At home, I showered again and sat on the couch in silence, smoking a joint. I tried to feel sad for Elizabeth, but I only felt empty. I thought about that asshole putting a gun to Elizabeth's temple and squeezing the trigger. The old cliché—if I can't have her, no one can. Elizabeth's boyfriend knew she'd dump him and forget him once she got to college. That's the way things always happen here. When someone gets out, she rarely comes back. In a way I knew that guy's frustration.

Colleen and I rode around later. An hour passed before I said, "The car's in the shop."

"What car?"

"The Cutlass, you know, the one Elizabeth—"

"I wanna see it."

"Why?"

"I don't know," she said. "I just wanna see the last place my friend was alive."

"It's as hollow as a tin can now."

"What's gonna happen to it?"

"After we fix it back up, the bank's gonna resell it, why?"

"I want it."

I glanced at her and then back at the road.

"I'll just need to take over payments, right? I can sell my car and work while I'm at school."

I shrugged my shoulders, trying to act nonchalant.

"I want Elizabeth's memory to be all around me up there so I won't keep it inside," she said.

Thinking about her driving around in that car gave me the creeps. "There's a WVU catalogue in the glove box," I said. "I found it in the Cutlass."

She pulled the book out.

"There's a picture of Elizabeth in it."

She found the picture and looked at it. "She was so pretty."

"Look at the pictures in the catalogue."

She started turning pages and stopped at a picture. "My god," she said.

"Keep looking."

She flipped through the pages, gasping at times, shaking her head. "He was nuts."

"You buy this car," I said, "and you're gonna feel every one of those pistols pointing at you."

She glared at me a few moments and threw the catalogue out the window. The pages flapping in the air sounded like the wings of a hundred birds.

In the shop, she crept toward the car. I waited, watched. She opened the Cutlass's door and climbed in, shutting the door behind her. I walked to her. Inside the car, Colleen was on her knees, straddling the bare metal transmission hump. Her eyes slowly panned the ceiling, the dashboard, the floorboard. "Where's the interior?"

"In the trash."

She reached up and pushed her finger against the wobbly metal roof. "Imagine this being the last place you know," she said and punched the roof, leaving a dent, a fossil of her anger. "Dammit." She held her fist in her lap, shoulders slumped. That was as vulnerable and beautiful as I had ever seen her, and I wanted to cry for her because of her sadness, and I wanted to cry for myself because she was leaving me.

"Help me out," she said.

I took her other hand, led her out. The knuckles on her right hand were red, but the skin wasn't broken, nor were any bones. I kissed the warm flesh there. I kissed her along the wrist, the soft, white skin on the inside of her elbow. She put her other arm around me. I unbuttoned her shirt and sat her down in the car. The shocks groaned a little. I laid her across the transmission hump, her spine popping and cracking like distant gunfire. I started undoing her jeans.

"Wouldn't it be something," I said, two of her buttons loosened.

"What?" she whispered, her bare stomach rising and falling.

"If you got pregnant. In here."

She grabbed my wrist. "No," she said, and sat up. "No, not in here." She pushed me aside and scrambled past me, refastening her jeans. She stopped outside the car, looked in at me. "You're crazy, Allen," she said and hurried to the front of the shop and re-buttoned her blouse.

I sat there a moment, my breathing loud inside the car.

"Take me home," she called from the front of the shop.

I climbed out. She was silhouetted against the front windows, looking out into the darkness, her back to me.

Around one a.m., there was a knock at my apartment door. I climbed out of bed and noticed my erection from a dream whose narrative thread I'd already lost. I stood at the door. "Who is it?"

"Me," Colleen said from the other side. I grew even stiffer and let her in. She looked at my crotch, shook her head, and said, "Get dressed." I did, and she took my arm and led me to her car.

We pulled in the shop's parking lot. "I'm gonna get rid of it," she said.

"The car? Why?"

"I don't want anyone else to have it."

"What difference does it make?"

"It would desecrate her," she said. "Some couple parking in it. Someone like you."

"I'm sorry," I said. "I don't know what came over me. I—"

"Jesus, Allen," she said. "She died in there. How could you've wanted me to do that?"

I glanced at the shop, thought about the last two years I'd worked there, two years away from my old man. "I could lose my job," I said.

"Tell them I stole your key."

"You'll get in trouble."

She looked through the windshield, at Triple Oaks sprawled before us. "I don't care," she said. "I want to burn it, then get the hell away from this place."

I watched her for a few minutes and knew I was now part of something she would always associate with the death of Elizabeth—this place. All of it. The ridges, close together as corduroy. The roads, snaking, rising and falling. The town, buildings hollowed out, windows blank with plywood. The people, gaunt and quiet, their secrets and desires simmering, waiting for a fissure and then erupting. Me, my hands and clothes, and my mind contaminated by the car. At least I could try to redeem myself. The rest was too far gone. "I'll do it," I said.

She didn't respond. I watched her a few moments longer and climbed out.

Inside, I put the front-seat frame back together and we set it in the car. After bolting it to the floor, I cut a six-inch sheet of foam in two and placed the halves on the frame—one half as a cushion, the other as a rest. I opened the garage door and then started the engine. When I backed the car through, she pulled the door down and latched it.

She trotted to the passenger's side.

"I better do it alone," I said.

She leaned inside, studied me for a long moment. I felt warm in her stare and wanted to savor it for as long as I could. "You're gonna do it?" she asked. "Not just say you are, then finish fixing it after I leave?"

"Nobody'll ever get in this car again." I felt something warm climb my spine, and I thrust the floor shifter into drive and spun out of the parking lot, leaving her leaning against the back of her car, watching me. I knew exactly what I wanted to do with the car.

Two miles out of town, I took Crumpecker Hill at about seventy and was doing ninety when I hit Green Valley on the other side. All four windows were down, and the wind howled in the bare car. I pulled *The River* from my shirt pocket, popped it in the tape deck, and fast-forwarded it, trying to find "Stolen Car." The speedometer needle clipped a hundred as I ran the red light at the Oaks Mall intersection. On the south side of Summit, I slowed down and turned onto Oak Mountain Road. I serpentined the steep grade to the top, pointed the car toward Summit, and parked. A few seconds later, I found the song. A murmur of a guitar faded in, the tinkling of a piano.

There I was: in that parking lot atop Oak Mountain, where the tourist shop and Ridge Runner Railroad had shut down a couple of years ago. When the interstate and tunnel were finished east of Summit, the cars stopped coming by. For a while, kids came here to park and party, but the cops patrol it irregularly. Elizabeth was shot here. In this car, which now idled about fifty yards from the edge, as I hunted for a rock along the edge of the lot.

Leaning inside the car, I placed a piece of sandstone on the gas pedal. The engine revved. I leaned in and shoved the floor shifter from neutral to drive. The car lurched forward. I tried to leap back, but the door frame caught my right shoulder and spun me across the pavement, knocking me down. The Cutlass sped from the parking lot and took flight, the door flung open. Holding my shoulder, I stood and watched the car arc toward the treetops below, the motor racing wide-open. The car crashed into the branches, metal crunched, limbs snapped, glass shattered, and it settled to the ground. The engine died.

I crept to the jagged edge of the parking lot, where the nearly vertical embankment had long since given away, carrying a row of white guard posts and chunks of asphalt down the mountainside. The head- and taillights of the car had dimmed a little but hadn't gone off. The odor of steam, antifreeze, and burnt oil drifted on the wind. The hissing from the radiator slowly died out. Soon everything was quiet again, except for the engine pinging, the wind rustling the trees, and the occasional cars passing back and forth along the four-lane far below.

I walked back down the road and thumbed. A man in a pickup stopped and opened the door. "Awfully late to be hitching, ain't it," he said. He had on blue jeans, a black denim shirt, a bolo tie clasped with a shiny lump of coal, a tan polyester sport coat. He looked me over.

"I don't need a ride," I said and closed the door. He shrugged and pulled away, and I kept walking.

Two hours later I reached the parking lot of the shop. Dawn was breaking to the east, birds alive in the trees. Colleen's car was still parked there. I approached it. She was asleep, reclined in the driver's seat. I tapped on the window. She jumped, grabbing at the wheel. She blinked me into focus and cranked down the window. "Drove it off Oak Mountain," I said, "where it happened."

She watched me for a moment. "Your idea of poetic justice?" I stared at her until she started the car, shifted it into reverse, and I stepped out of the way. She backed around me, never looking at me, and drove off. She disappeared down Stanford Drive, and I could imagine the strip malls and fast-food joints falling away in her rearview.

By the end of the week, I'd lost my job. Though he claimed he hated to do it, Mr. Sommers had to let me go for wrecking the Cutlass. I was given a month's severance pay. Mr. Sommers talked the bank out of pressing charges and wrote me a good job recommendation. He didn't condone what I'd done, but he said he understood. I'd be moving back home at the end of the month, when my rent was up. I dreaded that, and the smugness Dad would greet me with, but I'd enrolled at Oak for twelve hours.

On Sunday, the day Colleen left for Morgantown, I didn't go to see her or call her to tell her goodbye. I spent the evening in my van on the side of that gravel road, where I'd told her I would be. Since dusk, I'd been sipping on the rest of the Canadian Mist I'd found in the Cutlass, hoping Colleen would do as she'd said—signal me.

Eventually, darkness settled in. The air was electric with cicadas and crickets. In the hollow below me, the mist was alive with the chimes of frogs rising from a small pond. I kept my eyes trained on the interstate. This was one of the farthest distances you could see around here. I concentrated on the taillights.

A little after nine, the lights of one car flashed off. It was her. I tried to judge her speed and visually follow her up the grade until her lights came back on. I scanned the road to the top of the mountain, her lights still out. I watched and watched. Finally her lights flashed on. I popped in a new copy of *The River,* turned the stereo up. Guitars and drums crashed the silence, releasing a Byrdsy arpeggio. A few moments later, still watching the lights, I started the engine, turned my van around, and looked away before she topped the mountain and disappeared.

her

She was leaning against my VW Rabbit, both hands tugging the hem of her T-shirt down between her thighs. Except for dark socks, the shirt was all she had on. Eyes wide, she watched me come closer, her face as pale as concrete. She had to be cold. It was early September, and nights in the mountains had already cooled, the trees tinged with yellow.

I'd just come from the Gallery of Kings, a dance club in Summit, ducked out after last call. I'd gone alone that night, without my buddies, who had dates. And I left alone, which wasn't unusual. Sometimes I'd meet someone there, but I would be with her for only one night. Now I wondered what was going on and why this girl was leaning on my car, out of all the cars along the street.

Stopping a few feet from her, I pulled my keys from my pocket. She was pretty, with black, shoulder-length hair curled the way heavy-metal chicks curled their hair then, back in '85. She had three studs in her right ear, a bracelet-sized hoop in her left. Blue eye shadow smeared her eyelids. Tears bled thick, black eyeliner down her cheeks. She looked nineteen or twenty, going on thirty-five. Behind chain link a few houses away, a mutt barked at us.

"Is this your car?" she asked.

"Yeah," I said. She had no bra on under the shirt, a black Molly Hatchet T-shirt, which she pulled down a few millimeters lower, taut against her nipples and ribs. On her shirt was a screen-printed Frazetta of a muscular, armored man gripping an axe with a large, rounded blade. The image was as cracked and faded as the frescoes we'd studied in my art history elective.

"Could you gimme a ride home?" she asked.

I watched her a moment longer and then scanned the other cars along the street, for some reason looking for someone else who might be watching, who might be waiting, laying for me. She seemed to be alone, but something had happened to her, something I didn't want to think about. I didn't want to get involved.

"Please," she said. "I just wanna get home."

Voices rose in the distance behind me. Laughing and talking loudly, a couple of drunks were coming out of the Gallery two blocks away, headed our way. I looked at her again. Her eyes were locked onto the drunks. She might have an even worse time with them than she'd already had with whoever did this to her. I'd seen those two inside, hitting on every woman in the place, grabbing the asses of some on their way to the restroom or bar. When those two saw someone leave a half-empty pitcher of beer to go dance, they filled their glasses.

"Where do you live?" I asked.

Still watching the two men, she gestured her head to her right and said, "Jenkins Street. Across the tracks, over the MLK Bridge." I studied Stony Ridge, the mountainside that rose above the halogen glow of the Norfolk-Southern railroad yard, which, until recently, had always served as the color line in Summit. Street lamps and yellow rectangles of light gave out about halfway up the slope. She saw me gazing across the tracks. "It's safe," she said. "Not everybody's black no more, if that's what you're worried about." Her shoulders were rounded, knees bent a little, as if she were ready to beg.

The men had seen her now and were picking up their pace, already yelling at her.

"Please," she said, watching them.

I hurried her to the passenger's side, unlocked the door, nearly shoving her in, and then hopped in my side. The car seat enveloped her, and she tugged her shirttail between her legs and pressed her knees together.

After I pulled away, leaving the men standing in the middle of the street, waving their arms in my rearview, she said, "I guess you're wondering about this." Her voice broke up a little, and she cleared her throat a couple of times.

"Well, yeah," I said.

"They raped me."

Gripping the wheel tighter, I asked, "Who did?"

"Two guys I was going to buy something off of." She paused, gave me a quick look.

"Did you know them?"

She nodded.

"You're not going to the cops?"

She didn't answer. Letting go of her shirt with one hand, she wiped her eyes. I glanced at her, my gaze drawn to her lap, which flashed light to dark as we drove under overhead street lamps. A dark bruise in the vague shape of a hand was on her left thigh. She caught me looking and tugged until her knuckles touched the seat cushion. Cutting my eyes back to the road, I fidgeted in the seat, trying to get comfortable, and swerved around a flattened dog on the street. I couldn't get to that house soon enough.

"They kept my money," she said. "And they threw my clothes out the window." Her eyes shifted toward her stretched shirt, the image elongated vertically, cracks in the image separating like parched mud.

"You gotta watch who you get in a car with," I said.

Looking at me, she leaned against the passenger door, her knees squeezed together, pointed away from me, as if the door were someone she could trust. For the next mile, we rode quietly down Triple Oaks Avenue. The Stones' "Some Girls" barely murmured in the cassette player, but I could follow the words. The beer taste in my mouth had begun to sour, as had the feeling in my gut, and it was all I could do to keep from tracing that smooth line of skin between the bottom of her thigh and hip and the cloth of the seat. She smelled like pot smoke and Right Guard and men's cologne and Armour All—a vinyl seat. A Camaro, I figured, or a souped-up Nova, or something. Never before had I regretted having a naked girl in my car. The post-last-call leftovers at the Gallery never interested me the way they did my buddies, but I would pick them up sometimes, especially if I were with my buddies and they were doing the same. I didn't date much either, not even the thin, pretty ones, because they required dates and more dates and time and attention, which I didn't have in me and, at the time, couldn't figure out why.

Then, there *she* was.

"Turn left up here," she said, nodding at the steel-trussed bridge that carried Jenkins Street over the railroad yard. The bridge's once silver beams had long since been blackened with coal dust and diesel soot from years of trains dragging coal from McDowell County to Hampton Roads. The steel grate decking droned under my tires. On the other side, she said, "Turn right and go one block. You can let me off at the bottom of my street."

"I can take you to your house," I said. "No problem."

"You don't have to."

"I've come this far."

She watched me for a few seconds, shrugged, and then placed the side of her head against the glass, the sharp curve of her chin cutting into the night. I turned up the street, which was marked by a wooden post with the street sign torn off, and climbed the steep grade. Shifting from third to second, I popped the clutch too quickly. She let go of her shirttail to catch herself, and I caught a glimpse of her pubic hair and glanced away. "Sorry," I said.

"Stop," she said, hiding herself again.

I slammed on the brakes, wondering whether I'd scared her.

"The lights are on," she said.

"What?"

"Turn around."

The houses on both sides were identical—two-story, nondescript but sturdy 1920s models, each with a hipped roof, a dormer in the center, and a covered front porch. The houses were set close to the street, which was lined with cars no fewer than ten years old. "Turn around. My mom's up."

"So—"

"Please. She'll kill me."

I backed into a driveway, turned down the hill, and stopped at the intersection. Gang graffiti, spray-painted in black, was scrawled across the stop sign. A solitary two-story chimney and an empty foundation grown with weeds and locust saplings sat in the corner lot to the right.

"Thanks," she said.

I shrugged, wondering how long this was going to take. "What now?"

"You can let me out. I can hide out till she goes to bed."

I wanted to get rid of her, to get this over with, but when I turned to her to agree with her, I saw chill bumps had risen on her thighs and arms. The crooks of her elbows were dark. I focused on the railroad yard ahead of us. Down this far, the tracks were empty. Up near downtown, coal cars coupled all night, the metallic crash fracturing the crisp air. "It's kinda cool out," I said. "You're not hardly dressed for it." I looked at her. "Wanna just ride around, maybe, and get some coffee or something? Hardee's drive-thru is open."

She nodded slowly, as though balancing her head on her shoulders took considerable effort.

"My jacket is in the back seat." I grabbed my suede jacket, which I didn't like to stink up in the smoky club, and handed it to her. She turned away from me, slipped into it, and zipped it all the way to her throat.

In Hardee's drive-thru line, a cop car pulled in behind us. I watched it in my rearview, glanced at her. She stared straight ahead. I checked the mirror again. Two cops talked back and forth, occasionally laughing. The car in front of us pulled away. I drifted forward, looking at the mirror, at her. Could they see her? She glanced in the side mirror, over her shoulder, and then at me. I checked the rearview again. Should I tell them?

As I handed her three dollars, the girl working the window saw her and glared at me. I grabbed the coffees, handed hers to her, and didn't wait for the change. Pulling away, I checked the mirror several more times, afraid the cops would follow. She sank in the seat a little, holding the warm cup to her chest. I knew at that moment that you're only a second away from being either a criminal or a victim at any point in your life.

We ended up at the old strip mines north of Summit, where kids liked to party and mud-bog in four-wheel drives with oversized tires, where car thieves brought stolen cars and stripped them and torched them, where couples parked. I'd brought several girls here myself, after meeting them in the Gallery, and it was the closest out-of-the-way place I could think of.

I pulled over at the first wide spot. I couldn't go much farther down the dirt road, which was gashed with muddy ruts too deep for my Rabbit. I turned off the engine, sipped coffee, and focused on the half moon in the crisp sky, well above the trees, whose branches would soon be bare. Somewhere in the distance, coon dogs bayed, and I turned toward her. The moon whitened the high, naked sandstone bluffs, which, fifty years ago, were underground until the machines came, blasted away earth and stone, leaving the rock face scored every two feet, as regular as lines on graph paper. I looked at her and asked, "Why my car?"

She lowered her gaze to her lap. "It was the only one that didn't have nothing hanging from the rearview." She blew on the coffee, sipped again, and swallowed hard.

I caught a glimpse of my eyes in my mirror and saw the moonlight glinting in them. "Why'd you get in that car with those guys?"

She stared into her coffee. "They hang out at the Gallery." Her eyes darted toward me and back to her cup, and I ran as many faces as I could remember through my mind. "You go much?" she asked.

"Too much," I said.

"Always by yourself?"

"Usually with my roommate and another buddy, but they had dates tonight." And I was glad, for her sake and mine.

"You pick up girls in there?"

I shrugged. "Sometimes."

She watched me for several uncomfortable moments. "You go to school?"

"Summit State," I said, glad she might be changing the subject. "I'm taking computer science."

"I went for one semester. Now I work at Captain D's and help Mom out with the rent. Since my bastard of an old man won't."

We went silent. The dogs were closer, barking, on the trail of something. Sitting here like this was awkward and futile, and I was tired, still a little buzzed and very worried about her, about being caught with her. Wondering if her old lady was in bed yet, I finished my coffee, rolled down the window and tossed the cup out.

"Don't do that."

I turned toward her. "Do what?"

"Throw that out."

Outside, fast-food bags and beer and wine bottles littered the ground, down into the edge of the woods. "It's like a landfill out there now," I said.

"Get that back."

"It's just a cup."

"Pick it up." She paused, her eyes losing their focus on me. "Don't you see what's happened?" Looking past me at the sandstone face, her eyes glistened and her mouth was pulled tight in a severe straight line. It was the closest thing to emotion she had shown and I couldn't stand looking at it.

"Okay," I said and climbed out. Fifty yards away, the dogs broke across the cut, six or seven of them, running, yelping, heading straight for us. I hadn't seen anything run past, but they were after something faster than a coon. Maybe a bobcat or a fox.

I watched them for several seconds longer and reached down for the cup. Beside a mashed beer can, a graduation cap tassel had been flattened into the dirt. I grabbed the cup, got back in the car, and dropped the cup on the back floorboard. She watched the windshield like television.

"Thank you," she said, arms now an X over her chest. I nodded. "What are they after?"

"Maybe a fox," I said.

The dogs raced past and then cut back down into the woods behind us. Though I was afraid of what might happen next, I reached for her and tried to pull her to me. I didn't know what else to do. She stiffened and wouldn't give. I squeezed tighter, her elbows digging into my ribs. I could feel her in my bulky jacket as if she were too small now for her own skin. A strange warm feeling rose in me, and I began to tremble. She remained rigid. "You think I'm poison, don't you?" I asked.

She sniffled.

"It's okay," I said. I felt her relax a little. Fifty yards down the cut, flashlight beams emerged from the woods, and I released her and saw the figures of four men following the dogs. They were likely liquored up, carrying shotguns. I thought about taking her to the cops again or maybe to the hospital.

"Don't let them see us," she said. "Let's go."

"We're okay," I said. "They're not worried about us."

"You wanna keep me here?" She wiped her eyes on my jacket sleeve, the hunters close enough now that we could hear their voices.

"No," I said. "I don't mean that."

"Why do you wanna keep me here?"

"I don't. I just mean we don't have to worry about them."

Staring at the men, she shook her head. "Take me home now," she said.

"I'm not trying to do anything."

She remained quiet. I watched the men for a moment longer and started the car, my headlights now on the hunters, who stood maybe twenty yards away, watching us. I u-turned and drove away.

When I got to her street again, she said, "It's the next to last house on the right."

I pulled up to the curb and shut off the headlights. The windows were dark. In the streetlamp's light, I could see coal dust from the trains had blackened the beige siding. The next house up the street was empty, the windows boarded with weathered plywood.

She unzipped my jacket, took it off, again with her back to me, and opened the door. "Here," she said.

"I'm sorry."

Staring at the dash, she said, "You can't help it." She climbed out, dropped the jacket on the seat and slammed the door. I watched her scale the steps of her front porch, the shirt uncovering the pale skin of her bottom. At the front door, she kneeled down and lifted the corner of a welcome mat. She stood, unlocked the door. Before disappearing inside, she glanced at me.

I read the address number on the house, 214, turned around in the empty house's driveway and rolled back down. The downstairs lights flashed on. Standing under the yellow glow of the porch light was a woman in a robe. She leapt down the steps, waving at me. I wanted to stop and explain everything, but before she could cut me off, I gunned the engine, killed my lights, and skidded to a stop at the bottom of the street. In the rearview, in a cone of streetlamp light, she stood, pressing her hands to the sides of her head. A trickle of sweat dripped from my underarm and ran down my side.

At home later, I knew I'd lie awake all night, worried a car would slow, headlights filling the windows of my bedroom, the engine stopping, the lights flashing off, and two car doors opening, a dog barking a few trailers down. How could I say it wasn't me?

I turned right and spun out. Pulling my headlights back on, I made a left onto the Martin Luther King Jr. Bridge, which seemed longer and narrower now, as if not quite wide enough for my car.

sarah's story

for James McMurtry

The trooper woke me at nine that Saturday. He was Jimmy Harmon, a guy I knew from high school, a guy I might have dated, had he asked back then. He told me they'd found my car, on its side, down in the woods off Pumphouse Road. I'd left it there last night after I wrecked, coming home from the Last Resort, a remote bar where Oak College kids hung out, the closest bar to my house. The six-mile walk to my home farther out in the country took three hours.

"Lucky you're still alive," Jimmy said.

Holding my arms out wide, I did a slow three-sixty to show him I was fine. "Not a scratch," I said, though my right shoulder was a little stiff and my chest was bruised. I clasped the lapels of my robe together.

"Sarah, we told you last time was the last time."

I'd heard this before, but I feigned interest. My eyes burned. My head hurt. And that sour taste of cheap bourbon on my breath. An earnest look of concern crossed his face, and not being annoyed with it was hard. "Come on, Jimmy," I said. "Nobody was hurt, right?" I glanced across the road at some cows standing in a field. The bruise on my chest ached.

Pulling his citation book out, he said, "I'm writing you up for leaving the scene of an accident." He filled it out, handed it to me. "It could mean your license."

I cradled the ticket in my palm as though it were a small, wounded bird. A breeze picked up and the ticket started to flutter. For a moment I wanted to let it fly away, but I squeezed it in my fist, a little stunned he'd actually written it.

He said, "We called a wrecker. Dannelly's. Might wanna check with them later."

"Mighty Samaritan of you," I said.

He started to turn away but stopped. "Saw your ex at the Cracker Barrel this morning. I didn't speak though. He moving back?"

"No," I said. "He's here to see Riley." He peered past me, inside, as if looking for Riley, my five-year-old son. "He's at Mom's."

"Probably a good thing," Jimmy said.

"Probably is."

He looked at my half-finished house, and I grew embarrassed by the exposed R-board and Tyvek building wrap on the dormers upstairs and on the sides and rear. Construction began about three years ago, but it slowed to nearly a stop once I got it under roof and somewhat livable inside. I'd gotten the siding up on the front almost two years ago, but that was as much as I'd done. From time to time, I do as much as I can, but I haven't been able to afford to hire any help. I never mention that fact, though. "When you gonna finish this thing?" he asked.

"Soon as I get time," I said.

"Be a nice one when it's done."

"Thanks."

He looked me over another moment and then turned and left. I closed the door on the cloudy glare from outside. The air was crisper than I'd remembered it being last night. It was still, too, gray as concrete block, the clouds grouted in place. A snow coming, no doubt. I like snow, a fresh snow anyway. It takes the drab off the wintertime mountains. After the leaves fall, the mountains look as though they need a shave.

I like a good wet snow that sticks to every little branch and twig, to the power lines, the tops of fence posts, barbed wire, the backs of cows. A snow that mutes everything.

Last night the sky was windy, and during the whole walk home, I kicked myself for wrecking. I needed that car for work.

I called Mom, told her I needed to borrow her car for a while, that I had a meeting with a client. She asked me where my car was, and I told her it broke down. She drove over and then took me back to her and Dad's house in Carthage. During the ride, Mom was silent, the radio was off, and the air in the car was as fragile as porcelain. She was letting the silence do the talking. "Awfully cold today," I said.

She glanced at me and then watched the road and drove.

At her and Dad's, Riley was with Dad, who was grading papers in his study. I didn't poke my head in to say hi, didn't want a lecture, but I could picture Dad in there—natural among the stale books, the soft-light lamp, the haze of his cigarette smoke, NPR playing softly, his UNC Ph.D. hanging on the wall. As a kid, I used to sit in the doorway and watch him, my knees corralled by my arms, my chin resting on the moon-white skin of my kneecaps. I used to wonder if what he did was really work, like many of my schoolmates' dads did.

Before she handed me the keys, Mom said, "You're not going drinking, are you?" The expression on her face reminded me of Jimmy's and made me just as uncomfortable. "I'm meeting a client for lunch," I said. "Maybe a glass or two of wine."

"Try keeping it to the amount before the *or.*" She dropped the keys in my hand. "Steve's supposed to be here at six."

Without a coat and in his sock feet, Riley came running out when he heard our voices. "Mommy," he said, running for me. I stooped to catch him and winced when he smashed into my chest.

"Riley, you'll get sick out here." I labored to pick him up and wondered how much longer I'd be able to do so. He weighed as much as a bag of cement now, except cement doesn't squirm and wrap arms around you. "Where's your coat?"

"That old coat," Mom said. "It's a wonder it doesn't unravel into a pile of threads at his feet."

"Where's your car, Mommy?"

I glanced at Mom. "It's only two years old," I said. "I bought it too large so we'd get our money's worth."

Up the block a bundled-up kid pulled a red-wagonload of firewood across the street, a man in a wool-lined denim coat following.

"Daddy's coming to get me here."

I looked at Riley again. "I know," I said. "You behave with him, okay?"

"Maybe I should take him to get a new one. That way Steve won't think *he* has to."

"No, Mom, I'll get him a new one. Maybe next year."

"Your breath smells like those bottles in the kitchen," Riley said. I could feel him shivering.

Mom watched us for a moment and said, "Riley, you should go on inside out of the cold."

I let him down and kissed his red cheek, which was as cold as ceramic. He ran back to the house.

"He'll tell that to Steve if it comes up," Mom said.

Tucking my hands in my coat pocket, I jingled the keys and sighed a little, scanning the yard to show her I was anxious to go. "Steve would be one to criticize."

"I heard he's changed."

I glanced away from her, watched the man and boy up the street. I didn't want to believe that about Steve, though thinking like that was cold of me.

"Are you going to be here this time?" she asked.

"No."

"You should, Sarah. Something seems different this time."

The wagon tipped as the man and the boy tried to drag it over the curb. The wood spilled. They righted the wagon, stooped for the wood. I looked at Mom. "What?" I asked. "How can you tell?"

"It's just a feeling," she said. "You know how I have these feelings."

Mom had always thought she was somewhat psychic. She had a bad feeling about my marriage to Steve, the end of which didn't take a fortune teller to predict. The man and boy reloaded the wagon, pulled it down the sidewalk, and disappeared around the corner.

"It's just a visit," I said.

My client was a new doctor in town, a Filipino. All our new doctors seemed to be Filipinos, and they were among the few around here who built houses that required an architect. Dr. Ko had bought a tract of land and had picked out a magazine house plan but wanted to alter it somewhat, adding a few rooms, deleting some, while trying to keep the same square footage and exterior appearance.

This is architecture in Triple Oaks, West Virginia: fitting round pegs into square holes and then keeping the builder from putting corners on the pegs. Mainly I do additions like sunrooms, Florida rooms, rear decks, master bedrooms with vaulted ceilings, and master baths with bidets and whirlpool tubs and glass-block shower stalls.

After three glasses of wine and haggling over my fee with my client, before settling on a number, I went to the wrecker yard, angry that I'd let Dr. Ko talk me down a grand. The slur I'd heard many local builders use—*L.B.D., Little Brown Doctor*—wormed its way into my brain. Somehow he knew I needed the job, and he played me, but a signed contract was good proof I could make a living at this. I could support myself and a kid.

I thought about what Mom had said as I signed the contract and shook the doctor's hand, which was softer than mine. The ache in my chest, though, at first relieved by the wine, grew worse, deeper, as if a domino effect had begun.

After the meeting, in the bathroom of the restaurant, I stepped out of my business suit, the one with the gray skirt a little higher above the knees than you'd get away with in an office. I let my hair down and tied it into a ponytail and then dressed in jeans, a Virginia Tech sweatshirt, and a parka before heading for the wrecker yard, hoping to look unfeminine enough to avoid extra charges on my bill.

The side of my Camry was crinkled and scraped. The top was dented where it had come to rest against a good-sized tree. Deflated, the airbag hung from the steering wheel like a tongue. The car started. The steering worked. The engine didn't smoke. The mechanic said there was only superficial damage and that it was knocked out of alignment but drivable. I'd been going only twenty, twenty-five, tops, squinting at the road, which snaked back and forth in front of me like a cut live wire. I'd yawned. The next thing I knew, the car was on its side, the top pressed against the large tree—an oak, hickory, I didn't know. You can't tell in the winter, the dark. I had to climb out of the passenger's door and leap down to the steep slope. Glancing deeper into the hollow, I leaned against the tree, patted its bark like you would a dog's back, and then scrambled up to the road and staggered home.

After paying the tow bill, and after the mechanic removed the airbag, I returned Mom's car, had the mechanic follow in mine. I parked her car, left the keys in it, and didn't go inside—Mom, Dad, Riley, Steve looming. It was more than I could handle at the moment. I drove the mechanic back to the wrecker yard and then went to the Moose Lodge to play cards with a builder, R. C. McClarity, and one of his foremen, Curley Paitzell. I'd worked with them on several projects; I play cards with them often, to let them know I'm one of them, that I can hang, that they can't get away with anything on my projects. They don't build something right, I make them tear it down. I imagine all the things they call me behind my back. I imagine them saying they've been doing this for years and don't need a woman to show them how. I imagine them saying all I need is a good fuck, and each one is the one who thinks he can give it to me. Giving them the chance is one mistake I've yet to make. All I need from them is to follow my drawings.

My mind wasn't in the card game. After losing around twenty dollars, I finished a hand and then bowed out and ordered a glass of red wine.

"How much that cost?" Curley asked, eyes dark as wet shingles. He looked as though he'd showered before coming out, but the faint scent of galvanized nails and roofing still clung to him.

"Three fifty."

He whistled, his eyes shifting back and forth. "Why?" he asked. "They got wine coolers for two bucks. Bought many a gal one in here."

"That's not wine."

"It's still booze, ain't it?"

"Cheap booze," I said. "Floozy booze."

"That expensive stuff only gets you to the same place them wine coolers do," he said. He killed his Bud, swallowed hard and glanced at me. I watched his fingers fish a cigarette from the pack in his shirt pocket. Then I left the flatulent sound of R. C. shuffling the deck of cards. At the bar, I drank and thought about Steve and Riley. People who knew me and Steve always said Riley looked like Steve's side of the family in his face. I saw the resemblance too; it made looking at Riley hard sometimes, but he favored my side in his eyes.

Steve and I'd split up not long after Riley was born. We were headed in that direction anyway. I was still in architecture school, down at Virginia Tech, my last semester of grad school. He was a bartender—college was never for him, but bars were. After the Sawyer Inn, where he worked, closed at eleven, he hung out with his coworkers at other bars downtown until they closed. I slept nights, he slept days. We communicated via sticky-backs and the answering machine. We were good in bed together, and because we were apart so often, our sex was even more intense, when we actually ended up in the same room at the same time. I know now sex kept us together.

Riley was an accident.

After the divorce, I got custody. Steve left for Myrtle Beach. He had visitation privileges, two weekends a month, but we heard from him usually only during Christmas and maybe one week after Labor Day and one week before Memorial Day. He was here two weeks ago. Here he was again, calling and saying he'd made a mistake. I wondered if he meant our breakup. Was he going to try to take Riley? I asked that question during several more glasses of wine. No way would a judge let Steve have Riley, not after showing so little interest in his son for almost five years, not after the jobs he'd been fired from for drinking up the profits, not after medical rehab, which I hoped didn't work.

I polished off that glass of wine and ordered another, my reflection in the mirror behind the bar broken up by liquor bottles, the pain in my chest finally dulling again.

Later that night I wound up in a garage with R. C. and Curley. We were all drunk. R. C. was showing us a car he was restoring, a '54 Chevy, unblemished two-tone blue and silver paint job. With cars, enough coats of paint and enough buffing can make the past look unblemished. I imagined all the ways I could ruin that finish—sandpaper, lacquer thinner, blowtorch, concrete blocks from a bridge, a shotgun blast that could turn the hood into a large cheese grater. I grabbed the fifth from Curley, took a big swig. After lighting a cigarette, he started looking around for an ashtray.

"Ain't got one," R. C. said. "Usually too many flammable fumes in here."

Curley studied something in a corner, went to it. He picked up a two-by-twelve, about two feet long. He came to me, took the fifth, and handed me the board. "Hold this," he said. I grabbed one end of the board and let the other end fall to the floor. He took a pull from the fifth, wiped his mouth on his sleeve, handed the bottle to R. C., and disappeared, returning with a circular saw. "Hold it by both ends," he said.

I looked at him as though he'd asked me to strip.

"Hold it up, goddammit. Out in front of you. Wide part facing me."

"Are you gonna saw it in two?" I asked.

"Hell, no." He grabbed the board, my hand still gripping the end, and yanked it to arm's length, horizontal and level with my chest. "Right there," he said. "Now grab it at each end." I did so as he plugged the saw in and took another drink. Squinting, he looked me in the eyes.

I worried what he might do if I dropped the board. The blade could catch me in my breastbone, or it could jam and kick out and off go my fingers. But I held the board with all the steadiness my drunkenness would allow. It was just like high school, my always having to prove I fit in—moonshine in the parking lot before school; getting my old Bronco, crammed with guys, hung up in the mud down at Bull Falls; poaching cows with deer rifles up in Summers County. Why couldn't I just talk about a movie with someone or something? Why couldn't we sip wine and throw another log on the fire?

He fired the saw up, and it whined. After locking the blade guard open, he pointed it toward the board and, about one-third of the way from my right hand, let the blade barely kiss the grain of the wood. A slight rooster tail of dust kicked up. The vibration went all the way to my shoulders, and I tightened my grip, my palms sweating, splinters digging in. The pain in my chest vibrated back to life, and I could barely breathe. He slowly swiped the blade sideways across the middle third of the board and then back. Sawdust flew, clinging to Curley's blue work shirt and jeans. R. C. watched.

Keeping my elbows locked straight, I didn't flinch, didn't close my eyes. The room filled with the smell of scorched pine. Curley concentrated on the saw. He dragged it back and forth at least a dozen times, each pass shaving off barely more than the thickness of construction paper, and shut it off. My knuckles were white and numb, my fingers gripped so tightly to the two-by-twelve. My arms ached.

Watching me, Curley brushed the dust from his clothes, took the board from me. I let it go and tried to flex the tingling from my hands and forearms. The cigarette dangled from his lips, the ash growing long. He smirked a little, as though I'd just passed some kind of test, and then he looked at the board, showed it to me. He'd shaved a football shaped indentation about a half-inch deep into the wood. He placed it on the seat of a fold-up chair, flicked the ash into the depression. "Cigerrat?" he asked me.

I waved him off. "No thanks."

R. C. took one. They started talking about the car again.

As I left, they glanced at me but kept talking. Outside, I sat in my car a few moments, trying to settle my hands by gripping the steering wheel. I could breathe only in short, easy bursts. Riley was probably back at my parents' by now. All I wanted was to scoop him up in those blankets, warm in my arms, and take him home and tuck him in and watch his slow breathing, have breakfast waiting on him in the morning.

Dad answered the doorbell. "It's almost three a.m.," he said, trying to blink his mind into coherence.

"I came after Riley." Fists stuffed in my coat pockets, I tried not to shiver.

"He's staying with *him* tonight."

"Where?" I asked. "At his mom's?"

"A little late to be worrying, isn't it?" he said. He glanced at my car, took a closer look at me. "You did that last night?"

"Is Mom up?"

She appeared behind him, cinching her robe. "I am now," she said.

"Where are they?" I asked her.

"At his motel room, I guess."

"Which one?"

"The Comfort Inn," she said.

"You shouldn't be driving," Dad said.

"What if he took him?" I said to Mom.

"I tried not to let him take Riley," Dad said, "but there's nothing we can do."

"He has legal rights," Mom said.

"Kidnapping isn't legal," I said.

"He wouldn't do that," Mom said. "He wouldn't risk losing what rights he has."

"You'd better start thinking about what rights you have," Dad said to me. "You keep living like you are—"

"What kind of car did he drive?" I asked Mom.

"I'm not sure. A mid-size. Maroon, I think."

"He's going to get the upper hand," Dad said.

I started toward the car, yelled back over my shoulder, "I'm the mother. The mother always wins."

"Not when they're as bad as the father," Dad said. "Or worse."

I kept walking toward the car, refusing to say more.

"It had a sunroof," Mom said. "It was open."

"He won't have to steal Riley," Dad said. "Not the way you're acting."

I climbed in, inserted the key.

"In *this* weather," Mom said. "As cold as it is."

"He knows Riley's here most of the time," Dad said.

"He must smoke." She called out, "Did he always smoke?"

"Yes, he always smoked," I yelled back. Across the street a neighbor's light came on.

"And when he sees your car—"

"Sarah," Mom said, "you're going to have to give them room together."

Watching her a moment longer, I nodded, closed the car door, and pulled away, leaving them gaping at me from the doorway. Dad had always felt Steve wasn't good enough for me, so Steve was everything I was looking for at the time and, when we met, I fell in love with him, or the idea of him. But even when we started growing apart, it never sank in that I didn't love him as much as I wanted to infuriate them. Steve figured it out, though. When we were together, we may have been running from similar things. Then came Riley, a loose anchor trailing along behind us until he snagged on reality and yanked us from our shoring as we hurled ourselves toward nothing in particular. Riley left us stalled out with nothing but time to contemplate each other, ourselves, and recognize the vacuum that existed between us. It's a horrible way for a kid to be brought into the world.

I cruised the Comfort Inn parking lot and saw a number of cars with North and South Carolina tags, many with West Virginia University stickers on the back windows or rear bumpers. Then I saw a maroon

Ford Taurus from South Carolina. The sunroof was up. After climbing out, my car motor still running, I looked at the two rooms on the ground floor and the two rooms above them and wondered which one they were in. The night clerk wouldn't tell me, I knew, not as drunk as I was. My breath fogged, and my face stung from the cold. I wanted to pound on the doors but didn't. It wouldn't look good. Not in front of Riley. And Steve was here, after all. If he were going to kidnap Riley, he'd have been long gone by now.

I shoved my hands into the pockets of my parka and steadied my breathing. I got home after four a.m., took five Advils, and went to bed.

Next morning, the doorbell rang again, early. I focused on the clock on the nightstand—8:31. Struggling into my robe, I stumbled out of bed, my tongue trying to moisten the sour, cottony dryness in my mouth. My chest ached less now but was still sore. I opened the front door and saw two figures, one tall and one short, on the other side of the storm door, the glass partially glazed with a trapezoid of frozen sweat. It was Steve, with Riley. "Sorry I'm early," Steve said.

"How'd you find this place?"

"Riley showed me the way."

I looked at Riley and smiled, impressed and proud he could do that, but also ashamed I hadn't realized it before. Between Steve's car and the front door was only one set of footprints in the snow. I imagined Steve leading the way, Riley leaping from one of his dad's footprints in the snow to the next, the only blemishes in the smooth, white lawn.

Steve was studying me. "I'd like to say you look good."

I could imagine what I looked like—hair a mess, hung over. But Steve looked good, had put on weight in a good way, not as frail or pale as he once was. His face was fuller, making his nose seem a little small now. His hair was shorter than I'd ever known it, lighter from the Carolina sun. And those same foggy gray eyes many people around here seem to have. Eyes that make these people hard to read, until they explode, their pupils widened and black as ink. "How've you been?" I asked.

"Mommy, what happened to the car?" Riley asked.

"Someone pulled the road out from under it," I said.

Steve raised an eyebrow at me.

"First time it's happened." I tried to remember where I'd left my pocketbook, whether the ticket was still in it and not lying about someplace. I took Riley by the hand and pulled him to me.

Steve took a couple steps back and looked at the house. "It's gonna be nice when it's finished."

I nodded. "Hopefully by summer," I said. "Come in. Want some coffee?"

"That would be all right," he said. "But I gotta hurry. Wanna get down Fancy Gap before it snows more. I've gotta work tomorrow, too."

"Where?" I asked as he followed me to the kitchen.

"I'm a manager at a T.G.I.F. in Myrtle Beach."

"Manager?" I placed a filter in the coffee maker, filled it with grounds.

"I got an A.S. in restaurant management at Horry Tech in Conway."

"That's good," I said. "You should see the house this doctor wants me to do." I filled the coffee pot with water.

"It's sixty hours a week sometimes in summer."

"Wow," I said. "This house is two stories. Six bedrooms." I poured the water into the maker and turned it on.

"Big house," he said. "You wouldn't believe the amount of people from here I see down there."

"A master bath the size of that apartment we had in Blacksburg."

"They laugh down there and say Myrtle Beach is the southern-most city in West Virginia."

"When I finish the drawings I'm going to use them in my portfolio."

"Now, it's quiet. And flat. I'm not used to flat," he said. "Loneliness is worse where it's flat. I've been going to AA, though. It helps."

I looked at him. "AA?"

He nodded. "A portfolio?" Hot coffee sputtered into the pot. "Let me see it."

"Well, I haven't started it yet."

I thought I could discern a look of relief in his face.

"Soon, though," I said. "As soon as I finish this project I was telling you about."

He looked at the fireplace. Ashes from last winter still lay in the bottom. The block face was unfinished and charred, with corrugated masonry ties drooping from the mortar joints. Out back, collecting snow, was piled the stone meant to cover the fireplace. Also stacked back there was the cedar siding for the rest of the exterior, now gray as the mountainsides. "I see," he said.

"Staying busy," I said. "Only so much time."

"I should go," he said.

The coffee maker steamed and hissed. I watched Steve a moment. When we split up in Blacksburg, he'd only left a note, which said he'd next talk to me through a lawyer, but not to worry, he didn't want anything. He said he thought it was best for Riley. I should've cried then, but I didn't. I stared at the note and then at Riley, whom I'd leave with the university's day care during my classes and studios, and I'd think of all the possibilities that were out there for me and for Riley. I'd wondered what kind of person doesn't feel saddened when her own marriage has broken up. "Why'd you even marry me?" It was a question I'd always wanted to ask but never thought I would.

He looked at me. "You were different," he said. "Least I thought you were. I thought we'd end up different, not like everybody else—divorced, their parents raising their kids. But it was just the same. I may as well have married anybody from here." He turned toward the storm door, his back, to me. "Why'd you marry me?"

"Cause you were the same as everybody else."

"Probably should've asked these questions a long time ago, shouldn't we've?"

"Yeah," I said. I led Steve to the front door, opened it for him. You could feel the cold bracing against the storm door. "Hey, Riley," I yelled. "Daddy's leaving."

He ran in, and Steve stooped to pick him up. He stood and swung Riley around. Riley giggled. I smiled. Outside, the snow had tapered off but continued to fall from the gray sky. "We'll see each other again," he told Riley. "Soon."

"I know why you're here," I said.

He sighed, placed Riley on the floor, and kissed him on the forehead. "Sarah," he said, "I've been hearing about you. I'm worried."

"What?" I asked. "I'm doing fine. We both are." I wanted to get that contract with the doctor and wave it in his face. "I have work."

"I'm not talking about your projects," he said. "I never had any doubt about your work. You can make it on your own if—"

"If what?"

"If you stop."

"Stop what?" I asked, looking at him as if to say he was silly. "Stop drinking? Drinking has nothing to do with anything."

"Can you quit after just one, Sarah?"

"Yeah," I said. "The last one."

He zipped his jacket up, jammed his fists into his pockets. "You can do whatever you want to yourself—"

"It's just a joke."

"It's not funny."

"You're Mr. AA," I said. "Not me."

From the corner of my eye, I saw Riley watching from the cased opening that led to the TV room.

"Mom, am I going to Grandma's again?" he asked.

"No," I said. "No. Come here."

He came to me, and I stooped and held him.

"Am I going to see Daddy at the beach?"

I squeezed tighter, pressed my face into his neck.

"I should go," Steve said again. He turned the knob on the storm door. It rasped open, cold air rushed in, and the door slapped shut.

Watching over Riley's shoulder, through the storm door, I shook my head, afraid to talk because talking would turn into crying. The pain in my chest would worsen with crying, and I couldn't take any more pain. I stood and closed the door. Through the gap in the ice-glazed glass, I watched Steve stomp a new set of footprints to his car, fracturing the accumulation on the ground beneath his boots.

debts

A lot was happening the year I finished college. The Berlin Wall came down. The UMWA strike against Pockston Coal had turned violent, despite civil disobedience tactics by the union—a scab had been shot. My dad was involved in the strike, even though he'd been retired from the mines for a few years. He'd been arrested at a picket line in Dickenson County, Virginia, ninety miles from Triple Oaks, West Virginia, the town where we lived, but he kept going back, risking being thrown in jail again. Posting bail for him and thousands of others had cost the UMWA a quarter-million dollars.

In the meantime, I'd decided I didn't want to be a high school history teacher, for which I'd spent the last four years preparing—at Dad's expense. I was going to be a basket weaver. I'd been doing it for nearly a year and was selling a number of them on the weekends at flea markets.

After my commencement, Dad took me out to dinner to celebrate. He told me that he hoped I'd stay in the area to teach, to give something to the communities that really needed it. "Dad," I finally said, about halfway through the salads, "I've found a job."

"Oh yeah? Where at? What grade?"

"It's not exactly teaching, Dad." He set his salad fork on the tablecloth, took a drink of water, and pushed his plate aside. He laced his fingers together on the table. His hands were scarred and callused, and the black residue of coal was embedded in the contours of his prints. As I watched him, I rubbed the tips of my own fingers together, embarrassed at their softness. His eyebrows, gray and bushy, sagged on his forehead, the lines there creasing his age spots. It was difficult to look at him, but I cleared my throat. "I'm gonna keep weaving baskets," I said. "Full time. There's money to be made."

His hands formed into fists. "Travis," he said, "I didn't go in the mines just so you could weave baskets."

"I wasn't even born yet when you went into the mines."

"You was damn sure born by the time I put you through college."

I glared at him. "I'll pay you back, every cent."

"They was more than money put into it," he said, his stare driving mine to the corners of the dim dining area. He didn't finish his meal, but I did. I couldn't let him think he'd gotten to me.

After dinner, we drove home in a silence as fragile as a house of cards.

An Appalachian folklore class got me interested in basket weaving. A local craftsman, Bobby Costa, another ex-miner, visited for a demonstration. He'd been basket weaving since the long strike in '78, when he quit the mines out of frustration. Now he was his own boss. As he told us these things, he was cutting thin strips of hickory from a log and weaving them into the shape of the basket. His hands worked together with the precision of watch gears, weaving those hickory strips as easily as braiding hair. He spoke with the voice of a man proud of his work.

I watched and listened, my mind drifting toward my future, comparing it to the enthusiasm with which Costa worked and talked. I knew my heart wasn't in teaching. I wanted to set my own hours, work with my hands. I tried to make myself believe working with my hands would appease Dad, so I asked Bobby to give me lessons and offered to pay, but he said the tradition was more important than money to him. I talked

Dad into buying my tools—a variety of small mallets and steel wedges, even a crosscut saw for hickory logs—saying I needed them for class. While I honed my craft, my grades slipped. I'd spent much more time weaving than studying. But to keep Dad off my back, I still managed to student teach, graduate, and pass my certification exam.

Not long after my revelation to Dad, I leased a space in the Crafters' Mall, the old Kroger near the old bypass. The new Kroger was out by the newer bypass. Towns chasing bypasses.

I moved into the old Bluestone Hotel, now a HUD housing project, on Oak Street. They charged rent based on income. I reported mine as six hundred a month—what I'd made that April—until I could get a better fix on it.

A few weeks later, Dad began talking to me again, coming by the Crafters' Mall when he didn't go to the picket line, which wasn't often, but he remained ambivalent and spent most of his time with the ex–coal miners he'd discovered there. One carved miniature Christian figurines out of coal—manger scenes, the crucifixion, Jesus walking on the water—and one made mailboxes that were replicas of the state capitol building, complete with the golden dome our governor had recently spent millions of tax dollars on.

One day Dad showed up with a statuette—a carved, wooden figurine of a man riding a motorcycle. The piece was about the size of my hand, the detail perfectly rendered, right down to the rider's long hair, beard, flapping leather coat, and the bike's gas cap, spokes, straight pipes, and sissy bar. Dad had bought it for five dollars off of a one-legged drunk in a wheelchair—Claw Hammer—who carved things and sold them for liquor money. I'd seen him several times late at night somewhere along Oak Street, passed out, tipped over in his wheelchair, street kids laughing at him and nudging him with the toes of their shoes.

"Reckon it would sell?" Dad asked.

I told him it would; it was good-quality work.

"I believe this Claw Hammer's got some talent," he said.

I looked at him. "It's okay to be a crafter as long as you're a cripple?"

"It should only be a goddamn hobby for a healthy man."

I watched him walk away and knew there was nothing I could say that would change his mind.

Dad showed up the next day, wheeling Claw Hammer down the aisle toward an empty booth beside me, where a guy used to weld logging chains into crosses. Dad paid Claw Hammer's first month's rent, claiming he was going to help get Claw Hammer started so he could make something out of himself and sober up. Claw Hammer was a husky man. He had on a Harley baseball cap, his frizzy, black hair billowing from under it. His scraggly beard was somewhat grayed. He wore an Oak College T-shirt and cut-off blue-jean shorts, the pink nub of his left leg exposed.

He'd decided to make celebrity totem poles out of railroad ties—near life-size faces of famous people stacked on top of one another. "I prefer railroad ties 'cause of the creosote," he later said. "I can sniff them, cop a mild buzz, and make money at the same time." But he really used railroad ties because they were tough, hard to carve, but durable. After a while, the smell of creosote filled the entire mall, overwhelming my hickory sawdust and shavings, and the pine, potpourri air-fresheners, cedar, paint, varnish, leather, and lye soap that lingered around the other booths.

At first, I tried to ignore Claw Hammer, just to let Dad know he wasn't bothering me. Claw Hammer finally wheeled over to my booth one day and said, "Look, I don't know what the hell's up your ass about your old man, but me and you might as well get along. They ain't nobody else here for me to talk to but a bunch of blue hairs, Sunday school teachers, and crippled-up old miners." He smiled. "Cripples make for sorry conversation."

Claw Hammer turned out to be a good guy, fun to have a beer with at Lew's after work, easy to talk to. He even got us a few weeks of free beers when he carved a famous-drunks pole for Lew's: Dean Martin, Otis from *Andy Griffith*, Foster Brooks, and Norm and Cliff from *Cheers.*

He lived in the Bluestone too, surviving off government disability checks, and never reported his totem pole money. He was a former biker, who lost his leg when he wrecked his Sportster on the West Virginia Turnpike. He missed the big curve at the foot of Flat Top Mountain, near Camp Creek. Once, I asked him why he wanted to set up shop here and go into the totem-pole-carving business. "It's something to do," he said. "Besides, I couldn't let your daddy down, not after what he's done for me."

I sauntered back to my booth.

After a couple of months, Claw Hammer became the main attraction at the Crafters' Mall. He made a Cincinnati Reds pole, Statler Brothers pole, Creedence Clearwater Revival pole, Matthew-Mark-Luke-and-John pole, and a *Hee Haw* pole. He'd become so well known that the manager rented a billboard out by the Turnpike that read: *The Oak County Crafters' Mall: Come see Claw Hammer Colvert, the Famous Railroad-Tie Totem-Pole Carver, plus over 50 other crafters and mountain artists.* In the background was a diagonal picture of a *Gilligan's Island* pole. Claw Hammer had carved it for Bob Denver, who'd moved one county away to get away from Hollywood and be near his wife's family.

"That Claw Hammer's doing alright," Dad said to me once, more than a hint of gloating in his voice. "Ain't seen him out on the street in his wheelchair late at night, drunk, neither."

I could've burst Dad's bubble several times. Many nights I'd go get Claw Hammer from Lew's Place at closing time, just to make sure he made it home all right. On the days Claw Hammer decided to drink rather than work, I'd take him home or to Lew's in case Dad showed up. If he did, I'd cover for Claw Hammer, acting dumb, but I liked keeping that little secret from Dad.

In late August, Claw Hammer and I were in his booth, watching CNN. We were waiting for Dad to arrive to take us to the Norfolk Southern yard in Summit to get a truckload of railroad ties. Claw Hammer wore his pumpkin-orange "I Survived the West Virginia Turnpike" T-shirt, soiled with creosote.

A pretty young reporter said the strike in the Appalachian coalfields had become even more violent. She pronounced it Appa-*lay*-shuns.

"A second replacement trucker was shot and killed while leaving a processing plant near Van Sant, Virginia," she said. "So far, no arrests have been made." The news camera panned from her to a group of camouflage-clad strikers—miners and their wives—red bandannas tied around their necks. They waved cardboard signs at a long line of coal trucks. The reporter signed off, and the scene faded out and switched back to the main studio. Another pretty, young woman started talking about the reunification of Germany.

"What's your daddy think about all this?" Claw Hammer said.

"They'll come down on those workers like a hail storm of sledge hammers is what I think," Dad said. He was standing behind us, but we hadn't noticed. "Damn news. You can count on them to show a scab getting shot, but they won't show no troopers beating strikers' brains out with billy clubs."

When I looked back at CNN, more of the Berlin Wall had been toppled, the graffitied concrete beaten into rubble. Claw Hammer changed the channel to WVVA, the midday news. There was Bob Denver, who sometimes made guest appearances to do the local news or weather. He was also talking about the strike, cracking a joke about both sides digging deeper into the issues. And he hoped no one got the shaft.

"Ain't no damn wonder nobody takes us serious," Dad said, glowering at the TV. "Goddamn Gilligan."

Using the remote, Claw Hammer shut the TV off.

"Is this all y'all got to do down here?" Dad said. "Watch TV? Don't fit my definition of work."

"Just checking up on the strike," I said.

"Since when did you give a damn?" he said. "Basket weavers got a union now too?"

I glared at him until Claw Hammer said, "I made something for you, Mr. Blevins." He pointed behind his counter. A pole covered with a blue blanket stood there. He rolled his wheelchair to it and said, "Gentlemen, my latest masterpiece," and he pulled the blanket away. Four faces, contoured with wood grain and stained with creosote, were chiseled on the weathered railroad tie. The first was an old man with a high forehead, a thick mop of hair, and fat wavy eyebrows. Dad said, "Damned if it ain't John L. Lewis on top . . ."

Second was an old woman with scowling eyes; round, high cheekbones; a thin, flat, defiant line for a mouth; bun-tight hair interweaving with the grain of the wood.

". . . and that's Mother Jones. Even got the granny glasses! . . ."

Third was a younger man, bushy hair, round nose and chin, a heavy mustache.

". . . and Jock Yablonski." Dad paused for a second. "Hell, that bottom one's me." The last face had Dad's long, thin nose; crow's-feet; hair piled heavy on his head. Below him, vertical letters read *U-M-W-A*. "Why'd you put me on there for, Claw Hammer?"

"Well, I couldn't think of any other famous UMW people," Claw Hammer said. "'Sides, they ain't a damned one of them that's done more for me than you have."

Dad moseyed over for a closer look.

"It's my gift to you and the picket line," Claw Hammer said. "I been working on it a month or more. I was worried the strike might end before I got done."

"No chance," I said.

Dad kept smiling at it. I watched them a moment, feeling like an outsider. It seemed as though Dad had finally found the son he never had, one who adored all that miner shit. One who'd let Dad manipulate him.

An elderly couple entered the bay, wearing matching pastel-blue polo shirts, white shorts, and navy-blue orthopedic socks. They stopped at a pole that had Opie on top, Barney, Andy, Floyd, and Aunt Bea. Claw Hammer's *Open* sign hung from Opie's left ear.

"That one there's the *Andy Griffith* pole," Claw Hammer said and rolled toward them.

"Where's Ernest T. Bass?" the old man asked.

"Railroad ties ain't but so long," Claw Hammer said.

As he continued his sales pitch, I made my way back to my booth. Dad followed. "How much longer till y'all are ready to go?" he asked, hands jingling change in his pockets.

"As soon as I get the weave started on this basket. Gotta let its shape set up." I picked up a strip of hickory, wanting Dad to watch me. It wasn't necessary that I started the weave now, but I wanted him to understand the precision and care needed to bend and weave the strips in and out, horizontally around the dowels, to hear the wood strips strain as I bent them to near breaking. Once I had the strip worked back around to the beginning, I sawed off the last several inches to allow the two ends to butt together. I glued and nailed the ends to a rib and clamped them down with a small C-clamp.

When I looked up, Dad was examining a finished basket, running his fingers over the smooth, curving handle. "How much for this one?"

"Take it."

He removed his wallet. "What—forty, fifty dollars? I know you can't afford to just give one away."

"You can deduct it from my college bill."

"I'm serious," he said. "I'm headed to the picket line tomorrow. I might could pack some lunches in here for the men."

"It's a donation to the union, from me. Take it."

"Well," he said. "You don't mind if I slap some UMWA stickers on it, do you?"

"Do what you want. It's yours."

He turned the basket on its side and laid it on the counter top. He pressed both hands down on it, where the handle joined the basket, and mashed as hard as he could. It popped and cracked some, but it barely deflected. "Sturdy, ain't it?" he said, as though he were disappointed.

An hour later, we were at the Norfolk-Southern yard in Summit to get Claw Hammer's railroad ties. The yard smelled of creosote and diesel and coal. Heat waves emanated from the gravel, ties, and steel rails. To the right of the tracks, thousands of ties were piled in a dozen or so house-sized heaps. They looked like huge, upturned nests for birds as big as 747s.

Dad and I climbed from the truck and helped Claw Hammer out and into his wheelchair. He picked out about thirty ties that weren't rotted too badly or fractured from the weight of trains. Dad and I put on our work gloves and began dragging the ties to the truck, piling them near the tailgate. Once we had fifty, I slid a tie into the truck bed. Dad said, "Let me stack them. I know how to fit them in there real good."

I stepped aside, allowing him to climb in. I was used to his taking charge of everything, but it still managed to frustrate me. He grabbed the tie I'd just loaded, turned it onto its edge, and pushed it against the wheel well. I handed several more to him. He stacked them across the bed, and ten fit perfectly, just snug enough between the wheel wells to keep from sliding out. He paused for a moment, hands on his hips, as if to make sure I'd noticed what he'd done.

What I noticed was how Dad operated, so he could assume control of everything. I decided to see how hard he would work for Claw Hammer but not me, to see what he would go through to keep up this jealousy game, this anger he had for me. This need he had to be in charge.

I began handing the ties up to him more quickly, having the next tie ready before he finished stacking the previous one. After five more ties or so, I noticed sweat running from his hair, down over his face, which was flushed. He took off his work shirt and worked in his tank-top undershirt.

Off to the side, Claw Hammer fidgeted in his wheelchair, nudging his wheels back and forth.

By the time we had about twenty ties loaded, Dad's shirt was drenched and filthy. Creosote smudged his chest and stomach and covered his moistened arms. It was also smeared across his forehead, nose, and cheeks, where his dirty hands had wiped sweat away. He breathed loudly. I knew his lungs were weak from all those years of coal dust, and so were his back and joints and bones, but I kept hoisting those ties up. And he kept stacking, occasionally looking at me through squinting eyes. It had turned into a contest.

"Hold on a minute," Claw Hammer finally said. We stopped. He wheeled over to what was left of the ties. "A couple of them ain't looking too good after all."

"They were okay a minute ago," I said.

"See them ends there?" He pointed at one. "Starting to hollow out. Rotten inside. Be like trying to carve in a pile of sawdust."

I looked at Dad, now sitting on the ties, wiping his face with a handkerchief. His chest heaved. Beads of sweat glistened in the coils of white chest hair billowing from the V in his tank top.

"Let's find a couple more," Claw Hammer said.

When I carried one of the newer ties back to the truck, Dad was gazing up the tracks toward the main section of the yard. Lines of full coal cars waited to be pulled to Hampton Roads. "Half the Pocahontas field is on strike, and damned if the bastards ain't still getting coal out."

"Dammit, Dad, can't you do anything without thinking about that goddamned strike?"

"What's going on down there has something to do with *everything*," he said. "We're fighting for our pensions and our families' medical coverage."

"I'm your family." I pounded my finger into my breastbone. "And I don't get any of your medical coverage anymore."

"Basket weavers got health insurance now, too?"

"The hell with this," I said and threw up my hands and started walking away.

"Where you going?" he called out.

"I'll find a ride back."

"I was gonna take you to that sawmill over at Lashmeet," he said.

"What for?" I was still walking.

"I know a guy over there that'll give you a better deal on hickory logs than you get now."

I stopped and turned around. Maybe he was just trying to make me feel guilty, though he didn't have the same glint in his eye he had when he brought Claw Hammer to the Crafters' Mall that day. But owing him for something else was the last thing I wanted. "I've got all the logs I need for now," I said.

"We can at least go look at them, can't we? For the future?"

Was he making an effort to show an interest in my basket weaving? Or was he showing his approval? I feared missing my chance to experience that. "I guess," I said.

The logs were of good quality, straight, no knots, and they were fifty cents a linear foot cheaper than the ones I'd been buying. I scheduled a delivery for the following month. Dad seemed pleased.

His strike wasn't working out so well, though. The union had suffered thousands of arrests and, now, over a million dollars in fines. Meanwhile, Pockston held firm. The union changed tactics. They'd thinned the ranks at the processing plants to nothing more than token picket lines and began with roving pickets. Lines of cars and trucks, driven by strikers, inched along the highways and back roads, slowing the coal trucks to a crawl. Able to pull over only a few vehicles at a time, the state police had a more difficult time of breaking up the strikers. The strategy seemed to be slowly working. Pockston had begun missing delivery deadlines. The hope was to swell their coal stockpiles. The processing plants would have to stop. Then the mining. Pockston would have to agree to more talks.

By early November, after the autumn colors had dropped to the ground and browned, my business was slowing. I was told it would almost die until Thanksgiving, pick up until Christmas and die again until Memorial Day. My booth was teeming with baskets, but I continued weaving.

One day Dad asked if I needed money. I told him I was fine. I lied. I could pay rent on my apartment and eat, but my booth rent was going to be tough. I'd worked out a deal with the manager to make double payments next summer, and maybe one over Christmas. He agreed, knowing I'd done well the past summer.

"The manager told me about your deal," Dad said. He always liked to let me blunder waist-deep into my own lies before letting on he knew the truth. "Don't sound like being alright to me. All you make next summer pays for now."

I shrugged, eyed down the length of a strand of wood for trueness. It bent a little to the left, the direction it would be woven.

"Damn near like the mines used to be," he said. "Working to pay for working. You get scrip too?"

I forced the strip around a rib too quickly and it broke. I looked at Dad. "The rent's fair."

"Word has it the Board of Education needs substitutes," he said. "That flu going around."

"Word has it, huh?"

"That's what I hear."

I removed the broken strip, eyed another, and started it.

"Okay, I called down there to see," he said.

"Dad—"

"Son, you gotta work."

"I am working."

"Fine," he said. "But you gotta make money for it."

"I will."

"But what about in the meantime?"

"Dad," I said, "I can take care of myself."

He held his hands up as if to calm me down. "Alright. Alright," he said. "But it's something to think about."

"I have thought about it."

"What do you have against teaching?" he asked. "You started college wanting to teach."

I shrugged and focused on the strip of wood. When I was a student teacher, a month or so after I started weaving, I was sent to Shawnee, a small mining town in the west end of the county. Unemployment was high. The town had a reputation for violence—shootings, stabbings. Visiting high school sports teams dreaded going there at night.

The school was built in the twenties, brick neoclassical with stone cornices. Plywood filled broken windowpanes. Worn to dirt, the yard was covered with leaves, flattened paper Pepsi cups, and cigarette packs and butts. The day I arrived, kids leaned against the trees and smoked, watching me as if I were a cop. I entered with trepidation.

The principal, a man with a Shawnee Volunteer Fire Department windbreaker over his white shirt and blue-and-gold diagonally striped tie, met me in the office. He introduced me to the regular teacher, Mr. Shrewsbury, who led me to my classroom.

"Nervous?" he asked.

"A little," I said.

"They're mostly good kids," he said. "No different from those in Carthage or Triple Oaks."

I nodded and looked around. The chalkboard was flanked by an American and a West Virginia state flag. On the walls were pictures of Washington, Jefferson, Lincoln, the Roosevelts, Wilson, Truman, Eisenhower, JFK, Nixon, and Reagan. Also there was a long poster, a timeline of the significant moments in the state of West Virginia. Missing from it were the backgrounds of the earliest settlers, indentured servants for Virginia landowners, exported from the lower classes of the British Isles. Missing too were the Union and Confederate marauders after the Civil War had ended, the coal and timber companies' "land deals" with the residents, the Battle of Blair Mountain—

I tried to keep my cynicism at bay.

When the first-period class, a sophomore history class, entered, Mr. Shrewsbury took up homework, assigned reading, and handed out a study guide for the upcoming semester exams. He turned the class over to me and left, probably to smoke in the teachers' lounge. We talked about the Civil War, what had started it. During the first five or ten minutes, some volunteered their encyclopedic knowledge, others gave it when called upon. Several in the back merely shrugged. Halfway through class they were out of information. My lecture began, and I tried to fill the silence with facts and tried to keep my voice from trailing off, intimidated by their uninterested dazes.

Finally came the last class—West Virginia history. I wanted to fill in the spaces in that timeline on the wall. But most of these students, too, were uninterested, their gazes drifting toward the window, their heads lolling; others with their coats on, waiting for the three o'clock bell; a few girls in front, the good students, dictating everything I said into their notebooks. I stopped and looked at them. Pretty girls with big hair and too much makeup and clothes inspired more by the mall and The Nashville Network than by anything indigenous to the mountains. After a moment they glanced up at me. I looked at the boys, most dressed like Travis Tritt, mullets and all. The black kids tried to look like NWA. I knew the information I was giving them was just more junk from books, distilled into a language that made their home no different than anyone else's.

Inspired by Bobby Costa's visit to my class, the next day I brought in wooden strips and ribs for baskets. I went through each class that day anticipating West Virginia history, which I'd decided to secretly redefine as West Virginia folkways. Mr. Shrewsbury wouldn't mind—he spent the day out of sight. I made the kids put their desks in a circle and dumped the duffel bag of strips and ribs in the middle of the floor. "What do we have here?" I asked.

"Bunch of wood," one kid said.

"It could be considered a bunch of wood," I said. "Anyone see anything else?"

"Kindling," another said.

"Switches?" a third asked.

"It could be those things, too," I said. "But I see something else." I scanned their faces, which looked at me as if I were an alien. "I see baskets."

"Baskets?"

I pulled a finished basket from the duffel bag. "Some of these," I said.

"You made that?"

"Yeah." I nodded at the wood. "Out of a pile of wood about like that one."

One girl, one of the students who sat in front, raised her hand. "What's this have to do with history?"

"When did people used to make baskets by hand?"

"In the old days."

"When was history?"

"The old days."

"How many have heard your folks or your grandparents talk about the old days?"

Most raised their hands.

"Well that's where we're going." Feeling on the cusp of some sort of victory, I handed the basket to a student at the end of the semicircle. She examined it and passed it along. "Here's how we do it," I said and pulled a desk to the center of the circle. I took two ribs, smaller and more limber than I used for my own work, overlapped them, bent them into a basket shape and held it up for everyone to see. "This is the start of the frame."

I passed wooden ribs and strips to all the students, and when each one had enough material to construct a small basket frame, they all just looked at me. "What do you want us to do?" one of the smart girls asked.

"Weave," I said.

"This is stupid," another kid said.

"No," I said. "It's a part of our past."

"We can buy baskets at the store," said one of the quiet kids who usually sat in the back.

"These things break easy," said one of the troublemakers, snapping the strips in two.

"Don't break those," I said. "They're not cheap."

The kid beside the troublemaker started breaking his. I grabbed the strips and dowels from his desk and drew back to hit him. He stared at me defiantly. I lowered my hand and looked away. On the other side of the room, two kids were sword-fighting with strips. I went for them, tripping over the wood strips I'd left on the floor. They laughed. One girl left the room, came back with Mr. Shrewsbury. "All right," he said. "All right. Y'all settle down." He stared at me.

I laughed nervously. "Basket weaving," I said and stood up, holding a broken hickory strip.

"I see that," he said. "But what's the point?"

"History," I said. "Hands-on history."

He shook his head, ordered everyone back into rows, and took over the class for the rest of the period. I wasn't invited back and was glad. I told everyone that it was because of a clash in ideology. At another school I went through the motions of teaching, doing just enough to earn my certificate but without risking anything I really cared about, anything that would make me want to punch a thirteen-year-old.

At the Crafters' Mall, a few days after we'd picked up the railroad ties, Dad was talking to some other ex-miner. "That ain't striking," he said "Goddamn *roving pickets*. Gimme the old ways."

The other man nodded.

"That wasn't working either, was it?" I said.

They looked at me. "Give up too soon," Dad said. "A bunch of us is going back on the picket line tomorrow. And we'll by God stop those trucks before they ever get caught up in no roving picket."

"What about civil disobedience?"

"Time's getting too short for it."

Claw Hammer wheeled his way to us.

Dad said, "We're gonna set up Claw Hammer's totem pole at the front of the line. Show them we got a long line of history behind us. They just got a line of trucks behind them."

"Hell, I'd like to see that," Claw Hammer said. "An artist likes to see how folks take to his work."

“Then I’ll pick you up at six,” Dad said. He looked at me.

I felt I should go, to keep an eye on both of them. “I guess I’ll go too.”

Dad nodded and left.

“Your daddy’s a man that knows how to get things done,” Claw Hammer said.

“Like get us put in jail.”

“Hell,” he said, “it ain’t like jail ain’t no place I ain’t never been before.”

The next day we turned off of US 19 near Lebanon, Virginia, and drove the twisting back roads toward the tipple. From the ridge tops, through the bare trees, I could see mountains marching for miles in each direction, a few flattened and scarred by strip mines.

As we topped a steep ridge, I looked down in the hollow and saw the processing plant. Conveyors descended from the sides of the mountains, converging at a cluster of buildings, the tallest of which looked to be five stories. At the base of the buildings sat two round concrete cisterns, about fifty feet in diameter and filled with black water. Rotating skimmers raked sludge from the surface of the water. Huge piles of overstocked coal surrounded by front-end loaders were at the back of the complex.

The camera shots on CNN didn’t do the picket line justice. A lot more people than Dad had decided to forego the roving pickets. They filled the fifty-yard gap between the front of a line of coal trucks and the gate to the plant. The paved road was two lanes wide, and people covered every inch of it, spilling over onto the berms and embankments on each side, where the strikers had set up shacks and funeral-home tents.

At the bottom of the mountain, we had to park nearly a mile from the picket line. The air was cool and still, and dusk rose from the pits of the hollows. Shouts echoed from the entrance of the plant. Trucks revved their motors, and diesel exhaust hung heavy. I took Claw Hammer’s wheelchair from the bed of the truck. We helped him from the cab and into the chair, which we laid the totem pole across. I pushed, following Dad to the picket line.

Dozens of state police troopers and Pockston-hired security guards, all dressed in riot gear and holding clear plastic shields and nightsticks, had lined up in front of the first coal truck.

Once we got to the strikers, I stopped at the edge of the road. Dad disappeared into the crowd and came back out with a couple of men. The trucks sounded the air horns. Miners and their wives began lying down in the road. The two men grabbed the pole and headed back toward the front of the line.

"You coming, Claw Hammer?" Dad asked.

"You sure you want him out there?" I asked Dad.

"What're they gonna do, cripple me?" Claw Hammer asked.

"A man in a wheelchair might make them think twice about clubbing their way on through," Dad said. "And every second we win is a win."

Before I could argue, the air horns on the trucks screamed their final warnings, and smoke rolled from the blackened stacks above the cabs. Dad reached for the wheelchair. "I'll take him," I said and pushed him through the crowd to the totem pole. Someone had tied red bandannas below each face. Claw Hammer yelled, "Militant artist coming through," the entire way. We stopped. Claw Hammer locked the wheels of his chair and gripped its arms. We waited. The strikers grew eerily silent.

The trucks lurched forward. The riot troopers began edging closer to us, gripping their nightsticks, ready to strike. Their faces were hidden by the tinted plastic face guards on their helmets. When their shields were less than ten yards away, steadily closing the gap, I saw Claw Hammer's reflection on one, elongated, growing thinner and thinner in the middle, as though he were being pulled apart.

The cops launched tear gas into the crowd. Smoke poured from the metal canisters. The strikers erupted, screaming and shouting, coughing and gagging, but most people were determined to hold their ground. Only a few clambered out of the way. I pulled my shirt up over my nose and mouth.

Gas-masked troopers waded in. One of the pole holders went down.

Someone else, shielding his face with his arm, took his spot. A club thudded against a head beside me. I turned to see a miner's eyes roll back in their sockets. As he was about to collapse, two troopers grabbed him and lugged him into the concealment of the smoke.

A trooper grabbed Dad's wrist to cuff him with a disposable plastic strap. I yelled, "He's an old man."

The trooper hesitated, looking Dad in the face, and dropped Dad's wrist and yanked a younger man from the ground and cuffed him. Another trooper came, and they dragged the man away. Dad immediately lay down where the other striker had been. I released the handles of Claw Hammer's wheelchair and hurried to Dad.

When I got to him, I heard Claw Hammer yell, "They got the pole. They got the pole."

I turned and saw a trooper dragging the pole away. Two others lifted Claw Hammer out of his chair and carried him off. Right in front of me, a teenage girl clubbed a trooper across the back with a stick. The trooper turned, his stick drawn back. He saw she was a girl and lowered his stick and looked at me. I froze, as though my feet were tarred to the blacktop, closed my eyes, and waited.

Someone grabbed the beltline of the back of my pants and yanked me to the ground. "Stay down," Dad said. A woman, screaming and yelling, tripped over my legs. A work boot stomped my hand. Grunts, screams, and curses came from every direction. The troopers were winning. Flexing my hand, I tried to lay low.

A worker tripped over me. A trooper put a knee in the worker's back and cuffed him. I knew we'd get it soon, too, so I clambered to my feet and wrestled Dad to his, my arms wrapped around him from behind. "What're you doing?" he yelled.

I lifted him up and worked my way through the crowd. He elbowed and kicked at me, but I hung on. "Put me the hell down, boy." His sharp ribs dug into me, his flesh and muscle loose under my arms. He coughed hard, and his chest convulsed. Holding him in my arms, I suddenly realized how much of his physical life his work had taken out of him, leaving him arthritic, his skin and muscle barely clinging to his bones, his lungs choked.

After I got him out of the road, up the grassy embankment, and away from the smoke, I sat him down. Below us, several dozen more troopers, wearing riot gear and toting nightsticks, were emptying out of more paddy wagons and running toward the crowd. We could only watch as they arrested at least one-third of the strikers and beat the rest away from the road. The coal trucks passed through in a shower of bottles, rocks, bricks, and sticks. Once all the trucks were in the processing plant, the troopers closed the gates and stood on the inside. Paddy wagons began pulling away, full of strikers. The smoke drifted away. The totem pole lay in the ditch between us and the gate, less than twenty yards away. The bandannas barely fluttered in the air. Claw Hammer was sitting on the ground across the road, trying to beat the bent left wheel of his chair back into shape with a rock.

Dad finally caught his breath. He wiped his brow, drenched with sweat despite the cool air, and he looked at me. His face was flushed, thick white hair disheveled. Sweat ran down his cheeks. "I wanted out of there as bad as you did, boy," he said.

"Dad, we all get scared."

"Goddammit, that don't mean I wanted to leave." He rubbed his eyes with his forefinger and thumb and blinked a few times before refocusing on me. "You ain't the only one that can do whatever the hell he feels called to do."

"Dad," I said. "They're not the same thing."

The strikers were regrouping at the gate to try to keep the trucks from coming back out. Dad stood, brushed off his pants. "You go help Claw Hammer," he said. "Then take him on home."

"Dad."

"It's alright." He patted me on the shoulder. "The worst is over."

I watched him make his way back to the other miners and then turned toward Claw Hammer. As we worked on his wheelchair, behind us, a murmur started among the workers. Full of coal now, the trucks started up again and lined up behind the gates. “Let’s get over there with them,” I said.

“I heard that,” Claw Hammer said.

In January, the strike was still dragging on. Dad had been busted a couple of more times, and the union had spent into the seven figures bailing out its members and other strikers. Claw Hammer was still carving away, doing better than ever. After arriving later than normal, winter had settled in, cold and blustery. The second school term was starting, and I was sitting in the parking lot behind Triple Oaks Junior High School, staring at the brick building with aqua-colored window trim. Their regular eighth-grade history teacher had the semester off after also getting arrested; he’d flashed a woman at a photo booth, across the Virginia line in Graham. She got his license plate number and called the cops.

Thinking about what would drive a teacher to do something like that, I watched as parents dropped their kids off, the building swallowing them up. I finished off my cup of convenience-store coffee, stared at the school for a moment longer, took a deep breath, and followed the students inside.

red dog

It was late April, and John F. Kennedy was coming through southern West Virginia. Pax Combs toted a single-shot sixteen-gauge down a dirt road lined with Queen Anne's lace, daisies, and weeds that stood to his knees. In the sky, large gray-bottomed clouds occasionally blotted out the sun. Thin and stooped, Pax was nearly sixty, twenty years out of the mines and five out of Clover Pass Dairy over in Green Valley. He lived off Social Security and whatever he could shoot or grow or find, and he had a black-blue coal tattoo on the back of his crooked left hand from his last day in the mines. He wore faded, baggy jeans and a work shirt with a pocket patch that read "Buck," the pocket lumpy with 2¾-inch sixteen-gauge shells, lead squirrel shot. The shirt was too large, bunched in pleats around the beltline of his jeans, the sleeves rolled to above his bony elbows. He'd found it, a coat and a pair of hunting coveralls in a laundry bag in front of the dry cleaners in Green Valley. He had no more consideration for another man's laundry than he did for another man's land—he didn't think twice about ignoring a posted sign to go after a squirrel. He also didn't give a damn whether JFK was coming through here or not.

When he reached Clover Pass Dairy Road, he noticed a fresh sprinkling of red dog. The mines didn't waste anything, even these cinders coked out of the coal. Mines sold the red dog to the state, and every so often the state filled potholes with it on the back roads, especially this near an election. And this election was on Pax's transistor radio more than most had been. Just this morning, the news said a Humphrey man had complained that Kennedy's people were giving away free liquor and food in the poorer counties. The news also said Kennedy was giving a speech at Ceres School, where Pax had voted against Eisenhower in 1952, which was the last time he voted. He'd seen enough lies from all of them. Right now, all he wanted was squirrel meat, which was less gamey in spring.

To his right, something stirred the dried leaves. Pax stopped, shotgun poised, but he saw a yellow bird, a sign of rain. Overhead, a patch of clouds slid between Pax and the sun, darkening the road beneath the trees. Up a hillside too steep and thick with laurel to climb, a grouse drummed a log.

Pax rounded a bend and spooked a fox squirrel, which darted across the road, leapt to an oak's trunk and put the tree between itself and Pax. He aimed the gun, resting it on the back of his bad left hand, and cocked the hammer. The squirrel was higher up, hurrying along a branch, running out of range. He fired, but the squirrel sprung to the next tree, the branch dipping with its weight. Several leaves, shot loose, twisted to the ground. A chipmunk barked and buried itself under a log. "Damn squirrel," Pax said. He hadn't had meat in two days. Sulfur hung in the air, and the songbirds were silent. He reloaded and dropped the spent shell on the red dog, white smoke curling from the blown-out opening.

He crossed a low-water bridge over Stinking Lick and started up the next hill, feeling in his shins the jolt of his steps; in his leg muscles, the strain of the incline. "This here hill's the hardest part," he said, talking to himself as if he himself were another man he needed to encourage.

When he reached the downhill side, he heard a vehicle coming and then saw a glossy, black four-door Chrysler leading a billow of dust. Soon, before the November election, the state would spread dirty oil on the road to keep down that dust. Pax stepped onto the berm of loose red dog and waited for the car to pass, but it slowed. A lone man was behind the wheel, a U.S. Government license plate on the bumper. Pax knew he had something to do with that Kennedy. The car pulled alongside Pax and stopped, and a man half Pax's age stared at him through sunglass lenses dark enough to have been shaved coal. The man shifted to park and climbed out, leaving the door open, the car running, a black fedora on the car seat. He had a flat-top haircut and wore a white shirt and a black sport coat, pants, and thin tie. His black shoes were as shiny as the car. "Was that you shooting?" the man asked.

Hunting season was a long way off, and Pax was glad he missed that fox squirrel now. "Shot an old can," he said. "Target practicing's all."

"I heard you from the main road." The man took off his glasses, blue eyes focused on Pax. "Where're you headed?"

"Nowheres."

The man hiked the tail of his sport jacket back to reveal a revolver, and he looked at Pax's gun. "What kind of shotgun's that?"

"Sixteen gauge. Winchester."

"Good gun."

Pax nodded. "I'm pleased with it."

"Mind if I keep it for you a few hours?"

Pax stared at him. "Ain't no law agin having it."

"There is today," the man said. "With Kennedy coming through."

"Ain't got no interest in him."

"You a Humphrey man?"

Pax shook his head. "Him neither."

The man let his coat fall back over the pistol and looked at Pax's shirt. "Your name Buck?"

Pax glanced down and then back at the man and nodded. "I'm Buck."

"You even vote, Buck?"

Pax worried the man was going to charge him with contempt for not showing up for jury duty after the '52 election, also a reason he didn't vote against Eisenhower in '56: Pax didn't want anyone tracking him down. "I ain't voted since for Truman."

"Well, if you want to go hear Kennedy, they'll have food and refreshments for you down there," the man said. "*If* you let me hold that gun for you a while."

"I don't aim to shoot nobody."

"Funny choice of words," the man said. "But I don't *aim* to take any chances." He nodded at Pax's shotgun. "Now let me hang on to that gun for you a while." He reached for the shotgun, but Pax stepped back. "Hand it over, old man." The man uncovered his pistol again. Pax cradled the shotgun, shaking a little. Sweat beaded on his forehead. "Don't make me take it from you."

The man's eyes were squinted, and Pax knew this would be the first time in his life he might have a gun drawn on him. He shuddered, but blood also rose in his neck and face. A man ought not have his gun taken away like this, Kennedy or no Kennedy, but he figured he'd better cooperate.

Careful not to hold it too close to the trigger, Pax offered the gun to the man, who grabbed it and jerked it from Pax's hands, which dropped to his side, his good hand opening and closing into a fist. The man then stepped toward Pax, dug the shells from his pocket, and then shoved him in the chest with the heel of his palm. Pax's breath rushed out; he reeled backward and fell on his ass. He tried to inhale, but the breaths lodged like wads of wet clay behind his breastbone. Sucking for air, he rose to his feet and finally felt wind fill his lungs, each breath coming a little easier than the last. The man was opening the trunk to drop the shotgun inside.

"I'll need that back," Pax said, enough air in him now to speak. "It's how I eat."

"As soon as Kennedy is on his way," the man said. Pax watched him slam the trunk lid. "I'll be parked at the school." The man climbed into the car, turned it around and drove away, dust choking Pax as he followed.

When the clouds offered him a chance, he checked the sun for the time and knew it was after ten. Kennedy was due to speak at twelve thirty, if what the radio said could be trusted. Most things couldn't be, but a few could. Pax had been so lonesome he could cry, and he'd talked to his walls often enough.

The road bottomed out for a half mile along Stinking Lick, which was bordered here and there by birch and willow. The water was languid and brown, blotched with suspended clots of algae. The valley here spread a hundred yards across and was once a meadow carpeted with clover, which had long since been plowed under, but the road and dairy had kept the name. Low on the hills the trees were in full bloom, greener than the ones higher up which had just budded out. In the field, scarecrows with tattered clothes and pie-pan faces and hands stood sentry over columns of corn sprouts no higher than the roadside weeds. "Be plenty of corn come August," he said, spying the *No Trespassing* sign on the fence. "If I can get it before the deer."

At the top of the second ridge, he stopped to look at Green Valley below him, tractor trailers and cars inching along 460. Ceres School was barely visible around the last bend, where the road intersected Hurricane Ridge Road. People were lining the sides of the highway as if a parade were coming. Pax couldn't blame them. Now that he was here, seeing all these people, he kind of wanted to see this Kennedy, too, even though Kennedy might've cost him his shotgun. Before he started down the hill, he saw the black car, the man who took his gun sitting on the hood, his back to Pax. Here and there he could see a few more black cars and men in suits. Pax was reminded of the old coal camps when he was a kid—gun thugs everywhere. To the west, low dark clouds scraped the mountaintops, headed this way.

Pax's stomach rumbled, and he wished he had something on it. The corn pone and molasses he had for breakfast had already worn off. When he reached the dairy at the bottom of the hill, he circled around it to avoid the man in the black car. The air smelled like buttermilk, and he thought of crumbling stale cornbread into a glass, pouring buttermilk over it, and eating it with a spoon.

Over Stinking Lick, he crossed a black sewer pipe round enough for a bear to walk through. The water here was littered with old tires, refrigerators, a rusted Edsel chassis. Bleach bottles and tin cans were wedged in the branches of the overhanging trees, flotsam ornaments. The stench of raw sewage almost made him vomit, but he held his breath and hurried to the other bank. Where the pipe entered a concrete manhole, rust-colored slime leached into the creek. On the radio, Kennedy had promised he'd give the Appalachians money for water and sewer systems, new roads, schools. Pax wondered whether, for once, a politician might tell the truth. Hell, Kennedy *had* campaigned here more than anyone else.

Pax followed the creek to the main road, waited for a line of traffic to pass and hurried across as a car bore down on him. He glanced up at the grassy hillside above the dairy where pine trees spelled out its name, except vandals had cut down some of the trees. The hillside now read LOVER ASS AIRY. Dead white pines as red as foxes were scattered about. Pax thought that kids these days needed more to keep them busy and out of such meanness.

When he spied another black Chrysler, Pax looked first one way and then the other, for some reason feeling conspicuous. The man sitting on the hood was talking into a walkie-talkie, holding a Double Cola. He looked like the man Pax had met back in the woods, except this one's hair was darker, and he was a little older. He saw Pax coming, spoke into the mouthpiece again, and sat the walkie-talkie down on the hood of the car. Pax eased by, glancing over his shoulder at the man every so often.

Passing the Rainbow Restaurant, he made his way toward the school, which was a half mile farther down Airport Road. Beyond it was the grocery store, the dry cleaners, a machine shop, a produce stand, and a barbershop. In front of the school were a few more black Chryslers and several more state police cars. Cops directed traffic into a church parking lot across the road from the school, people arriving from all over—Triple Oaks, Summitt, Shawnee, Carthage, Elmdale, and even from Graham and Stony Gap, Virginia. The air was noisy with car motors and horns, and it smelled like exhaust and rain.

Heading into the breeze, Pax saw white smoke rising from barbecue pits: fifty-five-gallon drums cut in half, filled with smoldering charcoal and covered with steel grating. Towering above the grills, a sign read, "Oak County Democrats for Kennedy." The Triple Oaks High School band was playing "Stars and Stripes Forever," the clarinets a tad sharp, even to Pax's ears.

Pax fell in line behind a man who was about his age and who wore a straw cowboy hat and a beige corduroy blazer with oval patches on the elbows. His gut pushed a yellowed T-shirt through the unbuttoned flaps of the blazer. "That food free like they say?" Pax asked.

The man nodded. "I walked clean down here from Hurricane Ridge. I heared Kennedy's people's a-giving away liquor too."

Pax looked around but didn't see any sign of liquor.

"Ain't that just like a Kennedy?" the man said, stroking his wooly gray eyebrows.

Pax shrugged. Finally, he got to the grills and asked for a hotdog and hamburger.

"Well," the woman said. "Pick just one or the other." Her red hair was done up in a beehive, and she wore black horn-rimmed glasses and a blue and white plaid dress. "We need enough for everybody, and I ain't Jesus."

Before he could say hamburger, she gave him a plain hot dog on a cold bun along with a red, white, and blue napkin that read, "JFK '60." He moved off away from the crowd and made his way behind the school, where a stage had been set up, decorated with patriotic bunting. People massed around it. Hair slicked back, the men wore short-sleeve shirts and their bluest jeans, rolled up a turn at the ankles. The women were dressed like the woman at the grill, except many wore sheer scarves to protect their hair. Pax thought they all looked as though they were going to church.

Clouds were heavier and grayer in the sky now. The wind from the west had cooled. When the first drops of rain slanted to the ground, Pax looked for a place to stay dry. On the other side of Hurricane Ridge Road was an empty carport beside a brick house with no curtains. A rusted and faded tin realtor's sign tilted in the yard. He saw that other people had begun to migrate over there; eating his hot dog, he hurried, lest he couldn't find room among them.

Under the carport, he moved to the back and saw the old man from the food line. "Best to stand back here," the old man said, pointing at the other end of the structure. "Wind blows rain in from the west."

Pax finished his hot dog and crumpled the napkin up and dropped it on the ground. "You reckon that Kennedy's gonna stop?" Pax asked.

"I expect," the man said, nodding. "'Less it lightnings." He glanced at Pax and then looked at his shirt. "You Buck?"

Pax nodded.

"Gentry Alcott," the man said.

Pax wiped hot dog grease from his hand and shook the other man's.

Alcott's grip was firm and he pumped Pax's hand aggressively. "Good meeting you," Alcott said. "You a miner, Buck?"

"Was."

"Retired?"

"Got hurt." Pax raised his left hand up for Alcott to see.

Alcott shook his head and whistled. "No compensation, I bet."

"Nope," Pax said, shoving his bad hand back in his pants pocket.

"Kennedy claims he's gonna change that," Alcott said. "But we'll just see about that."

Pax nodded and looked toward the stage. In the breeze, the bunting writhed against the nails that held it in place. A gust picked up, sweeping JFK napkins over the schoolyard and across the road. One stuck to Pax's shin and peeled away when he shook his foot. He looked down at the red dye on his pants leg. In front of the school, the flags stood out straight. Thunder rumbled.

"Damn." Alcott studied the sky as if it meant to deprive him of something.

"You voting for him?" Pax asked.

"Hell, I don't vote. You?"

"Vote for *him*, or vote?"

"If you vote for him then you vote."

Pax couldn't argue with that.

People stood back from the charcoal pits as the wind whipped ash and sparks from the halved barrels. The clouds let loose the rain. Some of the crowd ran for cars, and the rest poured inside the school. In five minutes, the schoolyard was deserted. A milkman's truck, an old Ford step-side with round fenders and a split windshield, turned off Airport Road, drove past the carport, and disappeared around the bend, up Hurricane Ridge Road.

Rain slapped the aluminum roof of the carport, and people in front began to back farther in. "Whoa," Alcott yelled. "We packed tight as sausages back here." Someone said he was running for the school, and a man took off, a dozen people following, making more room.

"Wish I knowed where they was giving away that liquor," Alcott said.

Pax nodded again and licked his lips. He'd gotten a little food in him, so a drink sounded good right now.

For fifteen minutes the rain came in bursts, deafening against the tin roof overhead, and slacked off to a steady downpour. Alcott shook his head and looked at his pocket watch. "Twelve forty five," he said.

Pax was beginning to think, if not for his gun, he'd walked all the way down here for nothing more than a hot dog, but a state police car turned off Airport Road. Alcott tapped Pax on the forearm. "Looky yonder, Buck." Behind the police car was another black Chrysler, and then a white four-door Cadillac, the convertible top up, followed by another black Chrysler. The cars pulled off the road, the Cadillac stopping at the mouth of the driveway that led inside the carport. Two men were in front and two in back.

"It's him," Alcott said.

"You reckon?" Pax asked, as everyone bunched at the front of the structure, rain lashing them.

The car idled, windshield wipers flapping. Rain coursed the foggy windows. Suddenly, one window slid down, and there he was. Pax squinted, making sure. His face was much clearer than it was on Pax's snowy TV, no matter how much he'd fiddle with the rabbit ears.

"I be dog," Alcott whispered.

Kennedy smiled at the crowd of people under the carport, waved a little, his teeth white as something a rich woman would keep in a jewelry box, Pax thought. Before he realized what he'd done, he waved back and then felt ashamed of himself for acting like a teenaged girl who'd just met Elvis. Hell, Kennedy wasn't even president yet.

Thunder rolled again, and Kennedy leaned through the car window and glanced at the sky. He twisted toward a man who shared the back seat with him before returning a smile to the crowd. "My staff tells me I should cancel."

The people around Pax murmured. "Figures," Alcott said to Pax.

"Not to worry," Kennedy added. He looked at Pax and pointed at his shirt. "People like Buck there have come a long way to hear my message, and I intend to deliver it to you."

Pax wanted to yell out that his name wasn't Buck, but Kennedy's hand waved and the window slid up. Pax noticed Kennedy's arm didn't work a window crank and thought that a Kennedy didn't even have to crank up his own damn car windows. Pax remembered that, yesterday, the radio said Humphrey's campaign bus had broken down near Whitesville. People weren't going to be taken in by that, Pax decided, especially when Kennedy had a Cadillac that rolled up its own windows.

The wind picked up again, and the cars pulled away and circled in the schoolyard, kicking up mud clots. The rain now came straight down, pelting everything, percussive spatters and pings and drips. Pax glanced at the platform and noticed some of the bunting had pulled loose and was flailing in the wind, the white center stripe bled through with red and blue. In the school, people had crowded into the aqua-colored framed windows, staring at the caravan. The coal in the barrel pits steamed. The cars stopped in front of the platform, the Cadillac at its center, and they sat there idling as the rain continued to fall.

"They done stopped," Alcott said, as if surprised.

"Yep," Pax said, smiling.

A half hour later, the rain slacked off. Flanked by two black-suited men and wearing a long, black coat, Kennedy marched up the steps of the platform. The man flanking Kennedy's right held a black umbrella over him. Kennedy stopped at the podium and motioned the people under the canopy to join him. People filed out, and Pax and Alcott followed. "He's really gonna do it," Alcott said. Pax nodded, heart rate now keeping time with the rain pelleting the carport roof.

Kennedy turned toward the people in the school and cajoled them with a smile and a wave of his hand, which was now in a leather glove. Within minutes, the schoolyard was full again. Kennedy began speaking, but through a bullhorn because of the drizzle. "I'm honored to see so many of you brave this weather to come and hear my message," Kennedy said. "If I'm elected president, I intend to do everything possible to reward such loyalty." The crowd applauded.

He then talked about the Catholic issue. The radio had said Kennedy couldn't win in West Virginia—the state's just 10 percent Catholic. "Only 10 percent Protestant too," Pax thought, "but 80 percent heathen."

"When America chooses a president," Kennedy said, "it will be on the basis of his ability to fulfill the responsibilities of the office rather than on the basis of where he goes to church on Sunday."

Pax nodded while others cheered; growing up, he'd never believed what his Holiness parents said about Catholics—that they were all going to hell unless they got saved. Pax figured that a church that old must be doing something right.

"I say we let the issue of my religious beliefs die," Kennedy said, "especially when there are real issues to address, such as the hungry children I've seen in your state, the miners who get injured or laid off without compensation, the old people who cannot pay their doctor bills, the families who were forced to give up their farms, an America with too many slums and too few schools." This time, the crowd cheered a little louder, a few shouts and whistles breaking in. Pax particularly liked this part of the speech.

"Let me say this: If you in West Virginia vote for me, I will not forget you. I will invest money in your state to build an infrastructure that will promote development and new industries so you won't be a slave to the bust-and-boon patterns of coal." People cheered the loudest yet, a few *amen*'s even shouted out, but Pax wondered what the coal companies thought about this idea. A gust of wind blew Kennedy's umbrella inside out, but he didn't take his eyes off the crowd as the umbrella holder struggled to fix it and shield Kennedy again.

"In the meantime," Kennedy said, "I will double the amount of commodities available to the poor and unemployed. I will start the food stamp program that has languished under the current administration, and, until a new economy is in place in West Virginia, I will make sure that you get food." The applause was so deafening this time that Pax couldn't help but join in, his good hand slapping against his bad.

"Thank you and God bless you," Kennedy said, waving. The crowd erupted as if Jerry West had just won the NCAA championship game against California instead of what really happened. Pax watched Kennedy smile again and thought that a smile like that could help a man get away with a lot. The two men led Kennedy from the platform and into the Cadillac. The wind kicked up again, and the loose bunting flapped between the Cadillac and the car in front of it. The motorcade pulled away, and the bunting raked across the hood of the Cadillac, snagging on the antenna and tearing loose, smearing some blue but mostly red dye over the white paint. The caravan pulled onto Airport Road and headed west, the Cadillac dripping a trail of red spots, Pax imagined, like a gut-shot deer. A line of black Chryslers followed, and Pax figured his sixteen-gauge was in the trunk of one of them, but he could get another. Monkey Ward catalogue. Trap some muskrat all summer.

Someone tapped Pax on the arm, and he turned and saw Alcott, who said, "C'mon, Buck. I know where they's whiskey's at."

Pax followed Alcott up Hurricane Ridge Road, rounded the bend, and saw the milk truck idling in the drive of a house that had long since burned to the foundation. Budding blackberry bushes grew from a lichen-covered chimney.

They stopped on the passenger's side. Sitting behind the wheel was a lone man, bald on top and a bulbous nose dominating his face. Alcott opened the door, and Pax stood behind it, watching through the glass.

"Kennedy gone?" the driver asked.

"Yep," Alcott said. "Who are you?"

"Just a fellow who wants to make sure Kennedy wins," the man said, mustard-colored teeth clamping a cigar. Pax didn't think he sounded West Virginian, at least not from this end of the state. Hell, anything north of Beckley might as well be Ohio, as far as he was concerned. "You voting for him?"

"I am if what's in this truck is what I think's in it," Alcott said.

Pax noticed a few more men from the schoolyard were headed toward them, a hundred yards away. He glanced back in the truck. The man reached between the seats, and his jacket rode up his side. Pax saw a .45 in his belt. The man came up with two pints of Early Times and awkwardly reached them over the passenger's seat toward Alcott. "This oughtta be worth a couple of votes for Kennedy," the man said, his eyes red, his forehead high, greasy and creased. "Compliments of some interested parties, let's just say."

Pax stared at the whiskey, and the thread of Kennedy's speech began to unravel in his mind. He wanted his goddamned shotgun back now.

Alcott grabbed the man by the jacket collar, pulled him over the passenger's seat, and headlocked him, that oily head vulnerable. "Hit him with the door!" Alcott yelled.

"Goddammit," the driver said, feeling for his gun. Pax grabbed the handle and shouldered the wet door, driving the metal armrest into the man's head. Pax pulled the door back and shouldered it again and then again and again, banging it against the top of the man's head over and over, Alcott holding it in place until he dragged the limp man from the cab and onto the muddy yard, his head red and bleeding.

The men coming up the road were yelling, running at them. Pax took the driver's gun, stepped over him, and climbed over to the driver's seat, shoving the gun into his beltline. Alcott got in behind him. "Ha ha, Buck!" he yelled. "They's liable to be enough liquor here to last me and you two Kennedy terms." He slapped his knee. "Hot dang!"

Pax backed the truck out, swung it toward Hurricane Ridge, shifted into first, and mashed the gas pedal. The cargo bounced in the back—boxes of Early Times, he hoped. He wound the engine out and shifted into second, his good hand on the knob and his bad hand steering. The truck lurched over potholes and ruts. Some of the cargo crashed in the back, and Pax heard glass break. He thought he could smell bourbon.

"Not so fast," Alcott said. "We won't have none left."

In the mirror, the liquor man was climbing to his feet, the other men gathering around him. Pax shifted to third. Ahead of them, Hurricane Ridge loomed. Pax had never been up here, never had reason to, but he sped straight toward the mountain, shifting into fourth. He didn't know what was over there, and he cut his eyes toward Alcott, who broke the seal on one of the bottles, unscrewed the lid, and handed a pint to Pax, who tucked it between his legs. The old man opened another bottle for himself, and Pax took a long pull on the next straight stretch, where he could steer with his bad hand. The first swig was like kerosene in his throat and then the taste filtered in, sweet and harsh. He let it linger on his tongue for a few moments and slipped the bottle between his legs again, only his jeans separating the glass from the blue steel of the gun. Alcott knocked back a quarter of his pint, gasped, and said, "Goddamn, Buck, that's good."

The rain had slackened to a sprinkle. Kennedy was probably to Brasswell by now. From there, Pax didn't know where Kennedy was going, and he didn't care. All he cared about was now. He'd trade this goddamned .45 for a new shotgun.

The truck gained the base of Hurricane Ridge, where the pavement gave out to more red dog. "They's one after us," Alcott said, staring into the passenger's side mirror. In his, Pax saw a black Chrysler closing in. "We can lose him up at Wild Man's," Alcott said, "in the mud."

Pax felt the gun barrel in his jeans and wondered whether that driver's assault would even make the news, wondered what those Secret Servicemen would tell the tow-truck driver who'd winch their black Chrysler from the mud. Pax took another swig, wedged the bottle between his thighs. The truck slowing on the incline, he checked the mirror again, mashed the clutch, and geared down.

june hay

Whiskey bile coating the back of his tongue, Martin Cheatwood was sitting on the right-rear fender of the Massey Ferguson. Lawrence, his father, drove the tractor clockwise around an ever-shrinking perimeter of high grass. A high, white sun blanched the June sky as though it were August. Humidity slowly raked the ridges and valleys, silver leaf backs bracing against the air—a sign of a coming storm. It hadn't been forecast. The field was a third mowed, and a long rain could ruin the hay, but it was too late to stop now. His father wanted to at least get it cut and raked before the rain.

Yesterday, to make room for the new hay in the barn, and to keep last year's hay from rotting, Martin and Lawrence were supposed to restack the old bales and move them to the front. The new hay went on pallets in the back.

But Martin had been sitting on the front porch, staring at the barn, dreading the heat; the straw in his clothes cutting his skin; the ants climbing all over him, biting; the tired back, arms, and legs. His uncle Cooper stopped by. After being gone most of Martin's life, except for a few family reunions, Cooper had just moved back from Ohio, and Martin's parents didn't like it, especially since he'd taken a shine to Martin. Cooper was the black sheep, "the prodigal son come home,"

Lawrence always said. Cooper drank, a lot, and never had the same girlfriend twice. Martin couldn't believe he was Lawrence's brother, and he liked Cooper instantly.

"Just got a new cam on this thing," Cooper said and pointed at his '66 Impala, red and glinting in the sun. "Let's me and you take 'er out and see what she'll do."

Martin looked at the hayfield, the wind moving the waist-high grass in waves, the birds skimming the seeded tops. He looked at Cooper's car, the barn, a big hot dry dusty tomb for hay. "Let me leave a note," he said.

In the hayfield, Martin's job was to spy mockingbird nests woven in the tall grass so they could avoid cutting them down. As they mowed along the backstretch, a mockingbird swooped across in front of them, landing in the mowed hay. The bird ran across the fallen, freshly cut grass, dragging its wing, playing possum. When the tractor didn't bite the bait, the bird flew, dive-bombing Martin and his father, trying to ward them off. Soon after, Martin spotted the nest and told his father. Lawrence stopped the blade about a foot from it, raised the blade, and moved it past the nest, lowering the blade a foot or so beyond it. The mockingbirds quit chasing once the tractor was a good fifty yards away.

His father tried his best to save the nests. But, after the field was mowed, they were easily seen in the mohawks of grass by crows, chicken hawks, and house cats. His father said that even if only one chick survived, the pains they took to avoid the nests were worth it. No way could any of those mockingbird chicks survive the mowing blade.

Rarely speaking as they rode the tractor, his father talked only about the protective nature of the mockingbird parents, or pointed out the rabbits and groundhogs that eased into the field from the edge of the woods, the fence lines. He would say, "You gotta keep groundhogs thinned out, else they start digging up the fields. Cows'll step in the holes, break their legs," or, "Rabbits'll be thick out here come time the new grass and the clover sprouts back up."

His father's lessons had begun to repeat themselves, year in and year out, twice every summer when hay-baling time arrived in June and again in September. Martin felt as though his farming apprenticeship had become redundant. Now, after the trip to Ohio with Cooper, the tractor seemed even slower, the revolutions more and more constricting. Martin felt as though he could contour the rolling hayfield from memory, he'd been over it so many times. And traveling farther and farther inward, until the last square of grass, no larger than a pallet, was cut, wound Martin's boredom even tighter. He believed that if he ever sprang loose and straightened out all the revolutions of the tractor, he could go around the world. Linearity. He glimpsed it yesterday, a vast dose of it, while riding across Ohio with Cooper. On those long, flat, straight stretches, you could see an approaching car so far away its headlights appeared to be melded into one, until they split, the car finally zipping past several minutes later. Here, in Oak County, West Virginia, you were lucky to find a straight stretch long enough to pass in, the two-lanes were so curvy and steep.

"It's wide open," Cooper said, pointing at the flatness.

"Then why'd you come back?" Martin asked.

"Lost my job. Had to." Cooper bit the sentence off as if it were excess fishing line from a knot on a lure.

On the next revolution, as they approached the mockingbird nest again, his father veered the tractor to the right, arcing around the end of the strip of freestanding grass to miss the nest (the birds going through their injured-wing/dive-bombing routine again). The tractor left a shape in the grass like a mushroom with a crown the size of a kiddie pool. By the end of the day, a dozen or so mushroom-shaped stands of grass would be scattered across the field, until his father would meander the tractor around to mow the caps down, leaving the stems, where the nests were.

Martin shook his head and watched thunderclouds cauliflower the sky, not far away, and he wondered why those bird nests were more important than the hay, the cattle. He started to ask, but he knew the lecture. Cows were going to be butchered anyway. Birds are wild. That's the difference, his father would say. From his perch on the rear fender, Martin looked down at his father, whose head bobbed in sync with the motion of the tractor as it traveled the humps and rolls and pitches of the land. Martin felt he could finally read his old man, anticipate those pointless lectures. He was way ahead of his father. He scanned the ridges in the distance. A sparse tornado of buzzards twisted above Route 20. A dead deer, most likely. He glanced at the house, saw Cooper's car pulling into the driveway.

"Shoot!" his father yelled out and stopped the tractor, nearly throwing Martin. "Didn't you see that one?"

As two mockingbirds were attacking, Martin regained his balance. He waved at the birds as though they were gnats and looked to where his father's finger aimed into the mowed grass. A nest had been cut down. The eggs were broken, the yolks draining onto the grass.

"Sorry," Martin said. "I was watching Cooper."

"He's easy to see," his father said. "Now keep your eye out for nests." He put the tractor in gear and they traversed the field again without seeing another nest for three rotations. Martin scrutinized the grass, angry and wishing he had Cooper's luck.

Yesterday, no sooner had Cooper opened a fifth of bourbon, doing somewhere around eighty on US 35 near the Bob Evans Farm, a siren sounded behind them. Cooper pulled over. He screwed the lid on the bottle and handed it to Martin. "Slide it under your seat," he said. Martin did.

The cop smelled whiskey on Cooper's breath. "How much you had to drink, mister?"

"Just a swig."

"Get out of the car," the cop said. He made Cooper touch his nose with his head tilted back and his eyes closed, made him walk the white line on the edge of the road. Cooper passed the tests and got back in the car after the cop wrote him up for reckless driving—speeding twenty-five miles over the limit.

After Cooper started the car, the cop leaned in the window and said, "I'd have made you say your ABCs backwards, but you hillbillies can't even say them forwards." He grinned at Cooper and Martin, patted Cooper on the shoulder. "Get on back across the river," he said. "Where you belong." He stood and walked back to his car.

Cooper pulled away, looked at Martin, and grinned. "Hey, Martin? What separates West Virginians from assholes?"

"I don't know," Martin asked, wondering if this was the time for jokes.

"The Ohio River." Cooper laughed as if Martin had told the joke and Cooper had heard it for the first time. Martin laughed, too, but he felt a little uneasy about Cooper's recklessness.

"Get that fifth out," Cooper said. Martin did and handed it to him. Cooper took a long pull, passed the bottle to Martin. Martin looked at it for a moment and drank, his insides warming to the whiskey. The bottle was empty when they crossed the bridge at Point Pleasant and Martin tossed the bottle into the brown water of the Ohio.

On the metal fender, Martin's ass was stiff and sore. Cooper was inside the house, the best Martin could tell. The tractor descended a shallow dip on an eastern stretch of field near the woods, and Martin spotted a doe stamping its front hoof on the ground at the edge of the tree line, looking at them. "There's a deer, Dad."

"A doe. Must have a fawn close by, from the way it's acting. Warning it to lay low."

A spotted fawn sprang to its feet right in front of the mower blade. The teeth clipped the fawn's thin legs before it could run, before his father could stop the tractor. Everything silenced, except for the cracking sound of metal on sinew and bone and the shrieking of the fawn.

His father shut the tractor off. The fawn toppled over the blade, kicking its frayed leg stubs, blood spurting. It caterwauled like a calf, trying to stand on the jagged ends of its legs, but it could only flounder, smearing blood everywhere. The doe pranced back and forth at the edge of the woods, snorting, flagging its tail. The fawn finally collapsed to its side, its legs jerking in spasms.

"A fawn's taught to stay put till the last second," his father said, his voice as flat as a porch. "It's their one defense. They can't be smelled."

The sight of the blood, the sound of the calf, sickened Martin. After the exhaust of the tractor was blown away, the coppery scent of blood lingered. He almost gagged. "It's a crappy defense."

"They learned it before tractors." His father hopped off the tractor. "More times than not, it don't kill them." He slipped his Old Timer knife from its sheath on his belt, the reflection of the graying sky dulling the blade. "You wanna do it?"

Martin shook his head. "I can't."

His father watched him for several moments and looked at the house, but Cooper was nowhere to be seen. Before he left home for good, Cooper'd always taken care of these things. He could kill much more easily than Lawrence.

The doe pawed and snorted. "What about its momma?" Martin asked.

"She'll get on alright. Animals have short memories." His father stared at the fawn as if it were something about himself he hoped he'd never have to deal with. "I hope." After taking a deep breath, he squatted down over the fawn, which barely struggled. He pressed one knee against its shoulder, lifted its head up with his left hand, and placed the knife blade at the throat. The fawn bawled louder.

"Some folks say once a deer gets scared, its meat ain't no good no more." Martin turned his head. Still he swore he could hear the slice, like wet cloth being ripped. He shivered. The bawling stopped. "I never could taste no different though." Martin glanced back at him and tried to discern whether he was blinking away tears. "I reckon they all scared when you kill them."

The doe was standing motionless, its ears perked, watching them. It stood still and watched now that the fawn was silent.

"Go on!" Martin yelled at it. He couldn't stand to watch it watch its fawn get butchered. "Get on out of here!" He ran toward the doe, waving his arms over his head. "Get! It's dead!" The doe stamped the ground a couple of times, turned, and bounded over the fence from a stand still. It disappeared over the ridge, and when Martin reached the fence, the doe had stopped fifty or sixty yards down in the woods.

"Go!" Martin yelled. He climbed the fence, picked up a softball-sized rock, and heaved it at the deer. The rock flew about half the distance between them, thudded against the ground, bounced, and tore through the dead leaves like an animal burrowing. White tail erect, the doe loped out of sight into the woods.

As he turned to walk back up the hillside, he spotted his father standing at the edge of the trees, his silhouette dark against the whitish gray of the sky and the green of the rising field beyond him. He threw a rope over a low, thick tree limb, grabbed the dangling end, and hoisted the fawn from the ground. He tied the loose end to a fence post, the fawn hanging from its hind leg tendons. From that distance, Martin watched him gut and skin the fawn, steadily pulling the skin with one hand while shaving it from the carcass with his knife in the other, his mind maybe turning the animal into some machine part or piece of wood he was working on in the barn. After the hide had been cut away from the fawn's neck and flung off to the side, Martin headed up and climbed the fence. By then, his father was untying the carcass to carry it to the tractor. He gripped it by the hind legs. Gnats festered the wide-open dead eyes in the tiny head dangling near the grass. Flies buzzed the pile of guts and moist hide lying on the ground. It would all be gone by morning, eaten by coy dogs or possums.

Martin followed his father to the Massey Ferguson but heard a snort again, behind them, near the fence. Martin stopped and turned around. The doe stood there. Just as he was about to chase it away again, in the periphery of his vision, another fawn sprang from the tall grass near the tractor. It ran straight for its mother, leaped the fence in one outstretched stride, and the two of them darted into the woods, their white tails dissolving into the trees.

"It's the living that's important to an animal," his father said, almost smiling, as if the living fawn exonerated him from killing the dead one.

Martin scanned the field, crows already flying low over the fallen grass, pillaging the exposed nests and escaping with eggs or with squirming chicks in their beaks, the mockingbird parents chasing them.

His father threw the fawn across the hood of the tractor, climbed on, and started it. "You coming?"

"I'll wait till you get back," Martin said and walked back to the shade of the trees and sat down and watched.

His father shifted the tractor into gear. It lurched forward and crossed the field. At the bottom of the hill, he jumped off, opened the gate, and climbed back on, steering the tractor toward the house, up the grade. Cooper stood in the back yard, one hand shielding his eyes. Mockingbirds chased crows. The wind kicked up, brought with it the fragrance of rain. Flies scattered from the fawn's remains and then resettled. Martin folded his arms together and shuddered. Dark clouds overwhelmed the sky, and the hay lay on the field all around him.

the pillar of william's grave

Thunder trailed off, and Rachel heard T. R.'s truck climbing the driveway. She sat in the kitchen, sipping coffee. Stomping up the stairs, T. R.'s footsteps rattled the aluminum windows in the walls of their mobile home. Rain hammered the roof. Pushing through the front door, T. R. cradled something small, the size of a baby, wrapped in a mover's blanket. His hair was damp and messy. Two days of whiskers covered his narrow face. Drying mud caked his flannel shirt and blue jeans. "What is that?" she said, pointing at the bundle, but she knew, and she knew why he left for work three hours early, while it was still dark.

"Rachel," he said, "you gotta promise not to go crazy."

She approached him, reached for the blanket.

"Rachel, hear me out before you get any wild ideas."

She lifted a flap of the blanket and saw William, her son, who'd been buried three days ago. His eyelids were bruise blue, his skin greenly cold and rubbery. He smelled musty and sour, despite the embalmed scent that rose from him. His brown peach-fuzzed scalp was sucked into the soft spot of his head. She yanked him from T. R.'s arms. "Why did you do this?" she said, too angry to cry.

"I got to, Rachel," he said. "He belongs in the Lilly cemetery. I got lumber in the truck for a coffin."

"What happened to the old one?"

"Tore it up getting in it."

She bolted for the door, but he cut her off, grabbing her arm. "Is this how it's gonna be, Rachel?"

On her arm she felt her heartbeat under his grip. She looked him in the eyes, dark as wet blacktop. He released her, bit his lower lip, blinking away what appeared to be tears. Crow's-feet cut deeper into his face than she'd ever noticed before. He stepped to the door and jammed his hands in his pockets, looking outside. "I couldn't stand it no more," he said. "Daddy and Granddaddy both got buried in a town cemetery, and they don't neither one of them belong there. Not when five generations before them are in the old farm place." He turned to her. "I gotta start righting things now, or our land ain't gonna do nothing but turn into plain old dirt."

"Your family don't even own that land no more, T. R."

"I know," he said. "But don't worry none. It'll be over with soon."

"It was already over with once." She took William back to his room and laid him in his crib, where, last Sunday morning, she'd found him dead, his cold cheek to the mattress. SIDS, the doctor called it. Crib death, her mom had said. How could a child forget to breathe? And why did it happen on the one night she'd actually slept instead of tossing and turning, waiting for him to cry? She hated herself for sleeping, and she hadn't slept well since.

Now T. R. had forced William's death back on her, and she had no idea what to do about it. She was afraid to run, afraid of what T. R. might do—a man willing to exhume his dead son is capable of anything.

From her closet, she removed her good black cotton dress with the floral print that she'd worn to William's funeral. She took off her nightgown and panties and slipped the dress on, the long skirt falling around her ankles. She didn't wear anything else. She didn't want anything holding her.

In the living room, T. R. had hauled in two sawhorses, a half-dozen two-by-fours, and two pressure-treated plywood sheets inside, leaning the lumber against the couch. He looked at her dress when he came through the front door again, carrying his circular saw and a carpenter's L-square. "What're you wearing that for?" he said.

"They's gonna be a funeral, ain't they?"

"Out in the woods," he said. "We'll have to work in the rain, looks like. Better pack a change of clothes, some towels."

He laid a sheet of plywood on the sawhorses and measured rectangles. Then the saw screamed, sawdust rainbowing in the air. She turned away to pack the clothes.

An hour later, T. R. finished nailing the coffin together and they laid William in it. T. R. covered it with the lid, lined up the edges, and nailed it shut.

"We'd better wait till dark to carry him out," he said. The kitchen clock read 11:13. It wouldn't get dark until around seven.

She looked at T. R., at his eyes, as he stared at the coffin. Adrenaline coursed through them, widening his pupils like whiskey would.

The energy of his eyes had caught her up that way three years ago, when she met him. She was a hostess at the Western Sizzlin near the interstate. A tall, lanky Air Force private in his dress blues walked in, staring right into her eyes. Nervous, she glanced away from him and seated him in a corner booth on the other side of the dining area. But she felt him watching her the entire time he was there.

Finally, as he paid his bill, a wide grin stretched across his face, revealing his slight underbite. "I bet I'm causing chills to run up and down your spine, ain't I?"

"I just get nervous when somebody stares at me is all."

"You must get nervous a lot, pretty as you are."

She smiled and her face flushed.

"By the way, I'm T. R. Lilly," he said. "Private T. R. Lilly, USAF. And I'd fly a jet plane through that door there to get you to go out with me."

"What's T. R. stand for?"

He winked, said, "True Romantic."

They went out every night during his two-week leave and then wrote, constantly. The words in his letters lacked the energy of his eyes, but she felt them in the black ink scrawled across the paper. She could imagine lifting the strings of cursive writing from the pages and rolling them into small, glossy, black balls with the same dark sheen as T. R.'s pupils.

From his letters, she learned his real first and middle names were Terrence Rose, his grandfather's and grandmother's first names, respectively. She learned those names, especially Rose, embarrassed him when he was younger, despite his father's assurance that Rose wasn't just a girl's name. Look at Pete Rose, his father had said. Now, T. R. was proud of his name, even the Rose part. She learned he'd gotten so used to T. R. he decided to just keep it. She learned the history of his family and their farm down in Monroe County and that he planned to buy it back, start his own family there. Fate brought him to her, he wrote. She was the one to share that farm with him, and they would make sure that that land would only be in Lilly hands, and only Lillys would be in that land. Rachel liked the idea of being a part of a long family line. She was never really close to her own family—her folks split up and went their separate ways, leaving Rachel with her grandfather. He was moved to a nursing home once she married T. R.

But two years after they'd married, T. R. and Rachel were no closer to living on that farm than when he dreamed of owning it in his letters. They couldn't buy the land even if they had the money. The government had taken it for a camping area off of the Allegheny Trail. For a long time, T. R. left that fact out. Now he'd dug William up and was going to bury him on government land.

Standing at the living room window, she looked outside, at the mountain north of town, buried in gray mist, and wondered if the trees had reached up and grabbed the clouds, holding them over the valley, wringing out rain, as if God had instructed nature to make this day even more miserable.

In Monroe County, T. R. turned down a muddy road rutted with gullies. As the truck pitched and lurched, the coffin bumped against the inside of the bed and tailgate. It sickened Rachel to think William was bouncing around in that wooden box, his blanket unwrapping.

Overhanging blackberry branches scratched down the truck's sides. Tall seeded grass, water-glazed and bent over from the rain, sparkled between the ruts; then the truck mowed them down. They were stopped by a metal sign screwed to the top slat of an aluminum gate: "Authorized Vehicles Only Beyond This Point." The sign was riddled with bullet holes. T. R. swung the truck around in a wide spot and then backed up to the gate and shut the truck off. They hopped out.

"I'll have to carry it from here," he said, opening the camper lid and the tailgate.

"*Carry* it?" she said.

"It's alright," he said. "It ain't heavy."

He pulled the coffin from the truck and started toward the cemetery. She glared at him for several moments and then grabbed a pickax and shovel and followed him.

In the rain-beaten graveyard, she sat on a wet log. The woods were rich with the smell of rain and soaked earth and moss. She watched T. R. swing the pickax in the beam of a flashlight he'd placed atop a gravestone, glittered streaks of rain slanting in the light. A mountain laurel filled the background, its long, oval leaves bowed.

He pried up clumps of sopping mud and swung again, brown water splashing. He wouldn't stop to rest, as if stopping would give him a chance to change his mind. His waterlogged T-shirt was pasted to his flesh. As he worked, she watched his wiry muscles tense, contract, and then relax. Maybe his single-minded family pride would deplete with each flex of his muscles. How deep would he have to go before he'd toiled that pride away, piling it beside that grave in each shovelful of mud? She hoped he would dig to China, if that's what it took. He stopped about waist-deep.

"I thought it was supposed to be six feet," she said.

"That's for grown-ups." He climbed out of the hole.

Beside the grave, she dropped to her knees and looked in. Mud-clotted roots dangled from the jagged walls. The hole looked bottomless. She remembered a church flier about the rapture. In cemeteries, people wearing white gowns rose from graves, pulled through the soil, gleaned by the invisible hand of God. She knew it could never happen. There was a permanence to a grave. Only someone driven almost crazy, like T. R., could pull a body from the ground. God wasn't crazy.

T. R. grabbed the box by both ends and dropped it, splat against the bottom of the hole. A splash of mud sprayed her cheek. She wiped it off with her wet dress sleeve, grit scraping her skin.

"You wanna say some words?" he asked.

She remained on her knees, looking at him. "Who for, T. R.? Who for?"

"Suit yourself." He tilted his head skyward, closed his eyes, and clasped his hands just below his navel. She wanted to believe the water streaming down the bridge of his nose, over his cheeks, and channeling the lines in his face was tears, but she knew it was only rain.

"Lord, thank you for letting us bring William home," T. R. said. "Now let him rest in peace. Amen."

When his eyes fluttered open, she said, "I feel like we're criminals."

He glanced at her. "Sometimes the right thing seems wrong at the time."

After filling the grave in, he examined his work, a tired smugness in his face. He looked as if he'd just slickered her at something. She wanted to fight back. She stood and grabbed the pickax. Hefting the heavy T-blade high above her head, she turned toward a tall, thin tombstone behind her.

"What the hell you doing?" he said.

She swung the tool, stepping into the swing, and it clanked against the stone, knocking it cockeyed.

"Rachel, quit it. That's my great-grandfather."

She swung again, and this time a corner of the stone broke off, a brick-sized chunk. It flew several feet, landing with a spongy muffle on the wet leaves. She dropped the pickax and lifted the piece of stone from the ground and carried it to the head of William's grave. She fell to her knees and smashed the stone into the mud until it barely stubbed up above the ground. Her sopping bangs hanging in her eyes, she rested her hands on her wet lap and waited for a feeling of closure to wash over her.

"Ain't you got no more respect than that?" T. R. said, standing behind her. He picked up his tools and walked away. For a few moments, she watched him moving through the trees. Though she was wet and tired and cold, she felt a little stronger now.

She stood and looked at the engraving on the tombstone with the missing corner, its Gothic lettering barely readable in the dark woods: Terrence Lilly 1843–1907. Beside it stood a smaller, less ornate marker: Rose Lilly 1853–1939. Then there was Randolph Lilly 1862–1940, no wife buried alongside. She looked at the other stones: all Lillys. The dates started in the 1860s and ended in 1957, except for one: Aubert Lilly 1939–1970. It was the most recent grave, except for William's. She shivered, trailing behind T. R.

In the truck, Rachel took off her dress, dried off with a towel, and slipped her sweatpants on. She was unfolding her WVU sweatshirt when T. R. said, "Somebody's coming."

A pair of headlights roamed the field on the lower side of the road. Her heartbeat quickened.

The headlights wheeled around the curve, settling on them. She held her shirt to her bare chest. Rainwater running down the windshield glistened. The low beams flashed on. It was a white Blazer.

"It's a game warden," T. R. said, staring at the vehicle. There was a glint along the round edge of his eyes, which shone white as a crescent moon, taking the edge off of the dark gloss. "Kick the wet clothes under the seat. Let me do the talking."

The game warden pushed from the cab, pulling on a long, dark raincoat. He walked to the truck, and T. R. rolled down the window. "Got a license and registration?" he asked T. R.

"Yessir," T. R. said. The game warden shined his flashlight into the cab, across the seat, casting a yellow disc on Rachel's lap. He slowly slid the beam up over her stomach, stopping it where her arms held her shirt to her chest. She looked down at a faint shadow of cleavage above the blue material and covered it.

T. R. gave his license and registration to the man, who read the documents and said to T. R., "Ain't y'all a little old to be fooling around like this?"

"Well, you know how it is," T. R. laughed, "when the urge hits."

She felt as though she'd been slapped.

"Save it for the bedroom from now on," the game warden said, handing T. R. his license back.

"Yessir," T. R. said, and the game warden got back in his Blazer, turned around, and pulled away. "Nosey bastard," T. R. said and shoved a foot into a boot.

Rachel wriggled into her shirt and then glared at him. "Why'd you tell him we was fooling around for?"

"Had to get rid of him, didn't I?"

Rachel felt no more significant to T. R. than the tools in the back of his truck.

"I want the shovel," she said.

"No, Rachel—"

As soon as she was out of the cab, mired to her ankles in mud, he started the engine and mashed the gas pedal. The truck spun forward, slamming the open passenger door shut. The tires flung clods of mud, thudding them against her and pinging them against the gate. The taillights slipped around the black edge of the curve, and the drizzle on the ground soon swallowed the sound of the truck, the shovel likely tossed around in the bed.

She stood barefoot, alone in the rainy dark. If she had to, she would dig William up with her hands and carry him all the way back to Triple Oaks by herself. She felt as crazy as T. R. She scaled the gate, the aluminum slats cutting into the soles of her feet. Straddling the top, she heard the truck coming back. She wasn't going to let him stop her. She jumped to the ground. As she ran down the logging road, the engine shut off and the headlights dimmed a little. The truck door and then the camper lid squeaked open.

"Ain't no use digging him up," T. R. yelled. "I'll put him back again, sooner or later."

She tripped over a fallen tree limb and landed on her chest in the mud. She climbed to her hands and knees and paused for a moment, trying to catch her breath. She looked back into the headlights, at the truck door standing open. T. R. was silhouetted behind the gate.

"And I'm putting Granddaddy and my daddy back, too," he yelled. "And Mommy when she dies."

She stood and started into a trot and picked up speed, each step splashing mud and water. Her lungs and throat burned. Locust saplings and blackberry branches pricked and scratched her arms and legs. Her heartbeat and breathing fell into rhythm with her gait. She heard the drone of rain, the rustle of tree limbs, the wind rattling the fence wire on the right edge of the road. A strong gust lashed a cold sheet of rain across her. But her face was warm with real tears.

"You hear me, Rachel?"

The echo of his voice followed her around a bend in the road, out of the headlights' glare. She heard the clank of the pickax pounding against the padlock and chain on the gate. Each blow rang through the wet woods until the noise stopped and the gate rasped open. The truck started but she kept running. She had to keep running. This place had already consumed T. R. and swallowed William. If she stopped running, something vinelike would grow from the ground and encircle her ankles and root her there, holding her for those headlights to bear down on her.

margot

The weekend after Thanksgiving, my partner Harris James and I were remodeling the cabins of the Bison River Tourist Court in Jessup, Arkansas, one of those old spreads that reminded me of the roadsides along Route 66 in *The Grapes of Wrath*. The identical cabins were log, stained dark as railroad ties, with chinking discolored by weather and mildew. Inside, old V-notch knotty pine covered the walls. Real paneling—interlocking three-quarter-inch tongue-and-groove pieces of various widths—not the sheets of fake crap you can buy at Home Depot now.

It was not long after sunrise. A tool belt around my waist and under my denim coat, I carried a crowbar in one hand, a five-foot stepladder in the other. I was heading into cabin number four, which we were to begin gutting, starting with tearing out the ceiling tiles. We'd replace them with sheets of bead board to help make the units look more authentically 1920s, the look the tourist-court owner, Mrs. Suddeth, wanted.

At the entrance, I leaned the ladder against the front of the cabin, wondering why Harris hadn't left the door open for me when he'd gone in. He'd beaten me to the job site and had probably already started working. I turned the knob, pushed my way inside. Heat from the room blasted me in the face. Light from the doorway fell across the woman who was in the bed. She sat up and shielded her eyes with one hand. "What the—" she said. Her other hand was holding the blanket to her breastbone, covering her chest. "Who are you?"

"Whoops!" I said. "Sorry."

Pulling the sheet up to her neck, she squinted her eyes at me in the glare of the morning light.

"I'm remodeling the place," I said.

"Now?"

"Well, not this specific one," I said, in no hurry to leave, though I could feel the cool outside air blowing in around me and reaching for her. I looked her over. Her hair was dark and reddish, the color of stained cherry, done up in some kind of do that was disheveled from sleep. She appeared a little younger than I was, but not by much—thirty-nine, maybe forty. Even though she was hidden under blankets, I could tell she was short, no more than five feet tall. I took pride in my eye for proportions, for lengths and distances. I can eyeball the dimensions of any room to within six inches. Backing out, I said, "Came in the wrong cabin. Sorry."

She watched me but didn't seem a bit scared. "Be more careful," she said.

"You should lock the door."

"You should try knocking."

Those curves were naked under those blankets.

"You can close the door now," she said.

On the stoop, I nodded, watched her for a few seconds longer, and closed the door. I noticed her gold Saturn sedan, with temporary Texas tags and a dealer sticker from Fort Worth, was parked between numbers five and six, pulled in as far as it would go. From where my truck was parked, I hadn't seen it and wasn't expecting anyone to be staying in any cabin except number six—bow hunters from Missouri. The Bison National River runs near here. Public hunting, fishing, canoeing. The peak tourist season is March and early April, when the water's up from spring run-off. Then, the river is like a railroad track, trains of canoes floating it. The outfitters, stores, motels, and campgrounds all make their money over that five- or six-week period. By the end of May, though, the river is usually too low to float. Except for horseback riders and hikers, you have the stream to yourself. It's peaceful. The cliffs dwarf you. I always liked wading along the base of the bluffs, fishing. I felt small but safe there for some reason, the limestone hovering over me, the river coursing the base of it. And the river is full of smallmouth bass. If you know how, you can catch them one cast after another, until fall, when hunters take over.

"Over here," Harris said, standing on the stoop of number four. He was wearing his old army field jacket he'd had since Vietnam. He grinned as if he had seen the Saturn and had known all along that someone was in the room.

I headed toward him.

"You knew there's a woman in there, didn't you?"

He shrugged and said, "Not that it was a woman."

"Why didn't you tell me?"

"Well, since it's a woman, I guess I gotta help you get a date somehow or another."

"Let me worry about my love life, and you stick to carpentering."

Harris laughed again and disappeared inside.

An hour later in the parking lot, my circular saw was screaming. An eighteen-inch section of bead board fell to the ground. I shut the saw off, and the fresh-cut pine smell whisked away on the breeze. The air was a little warm for this time of the year, in the fifties, but the day was cloudy and windy. The clacking of the bare tree limbs on the mountains and the roar of the wind in the pines forewarned of a cold front coming down out of the north.

"Is there a good breakfast near here?" a woman's voice asked from behind me. I flinched and spun around to see the woman from number five. "I guess we're even," she said, smirking a little. "Sorry."

"It's all right," I said and checked her out. I was right about her height. She wore jeans and an unzipped emerald parka. Her hair was fixed now, but I wasn't crazy about the stiff waves. There were hints of gray, which didn't bother me, nor did the fact that she didn't wear much makeup. I was glad to see a woman here who was close to my age and who appeared to be unattached. "By the way, I'm Frank Powell."

She cleared her throat, looked away and then back at me. "I'm Margot. Margot Bailey."

"Good to meet you, Margot Bailey." I shook her hand, which was as soft as a woman's hair after she'd let it down for the night.

"Same here," she said. "Now about that breakfast?"

"Across the bridge," I said. "The Ozark Inn."

"Within walking distance?"

"Not more than a hundred yards."

In number four, Harris yanked furring strips from the ceiling, the nails groaning in the fork of his claw hammer.

"Good coffee?"

"Espresso, cappuccino, gourmet. A lot of yuppies come here from Kansas City, Memphis, Dallas." I glanced at her car. "That where you're from?"

"Are you saying I'm a yuppie?" Face flushing, I thought I'd insulted her and started to apologize, but she smiled and said, "I'm from Fort Worth."

"Where abouts?" I said. "I've been down that way a few times."

"Oh, one of those old suburbs." Her smile flattened, and she gazed at the mountains that surrounded town. "You know how they're all alike," she said. "Unlike mountains." She removed her hands from her coat pockets, put on a pair of horn-rimmed sunglasses. There was no wedding band. There was hardly any jewelry at all on her. In her right ear was a diamond stud no larger than the head of a ten-penny nail. And what appeared to be a thin, pink scar ran from the stud to the bottom of her lobe, as if an earring had been yanked out.

"Well, the Ozark Inn'll get you off to a good start," I said.

"I'm a little more interested in stopping," she said and headed toward the bridge. I watched her walk away and wished that bulky parka wasn't hiding her form.

After lunch, Milton Panas pulled into the tourist court and climbed out of his truck, and I could tell by his bunched-up eyebrows that something was up. He was bundled in his fur-lined denim coat, and he wore a plaid wool hat with earflaps, as if anticipating the cold front. Harris and I were working without gloves and coveralls.

"There was another one last night," he said.

"Where?" I asked.

"Near the Boy Scout camp. A cow," Milton said. "Just left it laying there."

"Bastards," Harris said. "Them elk ain't hurting nobody."

"Somebody's hurting them," Milton said and looked at me. "You still in Saturday night?"

"I don't see why not."

This was the fourth poached elk in Hayes County we knew about, and Milton was worried. Over twenty years ago, thirty elk were reintroduced to the river, transplanted from the Rockies, and a number of them died during a wintertime disease epidemic. Others were poached. Some people didn't mind, claiming those Rocky Mountain elk didn't belong in Arkansas in the first place. But most of the locals, from Boxley Hollow to the Bison's confluence with the White River, did a sort of neighborhood watch back then. The elk would ease into the field at dusk, easy targets for road hunters with spotlights. A gun shot, and the nearest neighbors raced to the scene and caught men dragging an elk back to their truck. The locals would get the license numbers and turn the men in. The law came down hard on them: jail time, confiscation of firearms, and huge fines, and the poaching mostly stopped. Soon after, the elk were immunized for the disease, and they were common all along the river now. DNR estimate was 170 animals. There was even talk of opening an official limited hunting season.

This time the poaching was worse. The animals weren't being killed for meat or even trophies; each was just left lying where an arrow had dropped it. The poachers weren't shooting from the road. They were riding dirt bikes and four-wheelers down the horse paths, miles from the access points.

It was a real shame, because this time of year, the elk are great. Mating season. At Baptismal Ford, people line the roadside and watch the animals in the fields. A bull elk's bugle is a sound you never forget, cutting through the chilled air like a warning signal. The bulls spar, locking antlers. They're not shy about mounting a cow before a large human audience, and you're not sure whether you're seeing something you shouldn't see.

Saturday night, Milton and I rode horseback from Jessup to Whitehead's Landing, on our weekly volunteer civilian patrol along the river's hiking and horse trails. We listened for shots, for motorcycle and four-wheeler engines. Milton helped catch those first poachers over twenty years ago, by then already divorced, still working at a wood products company in Harrison. His kids had all grown and were gone. His wife had decided she wanted a career of her own and went off to Little Rock to go to nursing school. Milton lived alone in the house where they'd raised their kids, on top of the mountain above Whitehead's Landing, near Mt. Tecumsah. The elk must've given him something to focus on then. I know for a fact you can't just sit around and obsess about what went wrong in your marriage.

The horses we rode were Milton's. He named them all, even the mares, after characters John Wayne had played. He rode Cahill. I rode Jack Cutter. We had shotguns in scabbards fastened to our saddles. In our saddlebags were first-aid kits, walkie-talkies, emergency flares, food, water, and in mine a flask of bourbon. Milton didn't believe that booze and guns were a good mix, but I liked a nip every now and then to knock off the chill.

That night was more December-like than the past few days had been: very little moon, a half coffee-cup ring. The limestone bluffs towering over the river cast their own illumination, the river washing along the base of them. Slack water lay against the opposite bank, where the valley gradually eased into the water, and the trail crossed the river every mile or so.

"The poachers been coming in off private land," Milton said, riding Cahill ahead of me.

"Somebody's gotta be letting them," I said.

We ducked under a low-hanging branch, holding our hats. The hooves of the horses were muffled in the sandy river-bottom soil.

"If it ain't somebody that owns land along the park," he said. "A lot of people are still mad about the government coming in and taking land like they did."

"Eminent domain," I said.

"Imminent trouble," he said. "But you can't blame nobody for getting mad about losing their land. Some of these places had been in people's families since way back before the Civil War."

We passed the shell of an abandoned barn, the stone foundation of a house, all abandoned in the early seventies. Broken-down fences and rotted posts lined much of the riverbanks. The horse trails were once roads to people's houses. Before the government took over, the fields around us had likely been planted with corn, pole beans, and tomatoes. Now the fields were overgrown with blackberry brambles, cedars, locusts, and bamboo.

We crossed the shallow water at a ford. In the warmth of my Gortex-lined hunting coat, I was lulled into the rhythm of the horse and into thinking about Margot. How would I ask her out? Where would we go? What would I find out if I got to know her?

A blast came from upstream. Jack Cutter reared up on his hind legs and whinnied. I held on. I looked down at the cold water swirling around Cutter's legs as if feeling for the right grip to yank the horse and me under. Strangling the reins, I struggled to stay on Cutter and watched the water. I imagined frostbite or hypothermia. Cutter dropped back to all fours and was ready to buck. Milton positioned Cahill beside Cutter, grabbed Cutter by the halter and yanked the horse's head to his chest. Cahill stood firm in the water. Milton leaned into Cutter's ear and said,

"Whoa, Jack Cutter." The horse snorted puffs of breath and flinched a little but seemed to be calming down. "Easy, boy." Cutter's breathing began to steady. "It's all right," Milton said to the horse. A few moments later, he released Cutter's head, hooked a finger through the brass bit ring on the halter, and led us across the river. Cutter was as calm as he'd been before we'd waded the river. Shaking my head, I asked, "The hell was that?"

"Beaver," he said. "Smacking his tail on the water in that deep pool yonder."

I shook my head at him. "Milton, why didn't you ever become a professional horse trainer?"

"If I had it to do all over again," he said, "I might of. You ready?"

I took a breath and shrugged. "I reckon," I said, now ready to concentrate more on the trails than on Margot.

Two hours later, Milton shone his flashlight on a set of dirt-bike tire tracks, curving from an old logging road onto the horse path.

"Looks awful fresh," he said.

"We'd have heard it," I said. In this canyon, with the air cold and still like it was, you could hear a motor for miles. "Probably from last night."

He nodded, staring at the logging road. "Let's follow it into the woods," he said. "Might be where they're coming in."

We followed the road to the base of the mountain, where the woods began. The road switchbacked up the slope, cut through a gap in the rocks, at a forty-five-degree angle, and topped the ridge. Below us, the river horseshoed around the foot of the mountain. The motorcycle tracks continued along the ridge top in the opposite direction of the river. We rode on. A couple hundred yards later we came upon another old barn, which appeared to be in pretty good shape.

As we approached the door, we caught a whiff of camping fuel and an acrid chemical smell, the horses flinching at the fumes. "Easy does it, Cahill," Milton said.

"Smells like cat piss," I said, remembering the odor from the litter box for Patricia's cat, which she had to get rid of after our first daughter, Sarah, was born and we learned she was allergic to cats.

"Smells like fingernail polish remover to me," Milton said, and I wondered what memory of his ex-wife just went through his mind.

We dismounted, tied the horses off to an old fence post, crept to the barn.

Milton shone his light inside. Scattered on the floor were several empty antifreeze jugs, red-stained conical coffee filters, dozens of opened allergy medicine boxes and foil-backed blister packs, hundreds of pills pushed through the foil. There were Drano cans, mutilated D-size batteries, and what appeared to be thousands of kitchen matches. I looked closer and noticed the heads were pinched off. A gob of amber, stiff as pinesap and enough to fill a fifty-five-gallon drum, lay in the corner.

"I seen this on the news," Milton said.

"The hell is it?"

"Unless I'm wrong," he said, "it's a meth lab."

"Methamphetamine?"

"Looks like it," he said. "Redneck crack. Hell, Hitler even made the German soldiers take it to keep them awake, to keep them fighting without giving a damn about their own selves."

We studied the gob pile a moment. Milton scratched his head and asked, "Wanna keep following the tracks?"

"We're after elk killers, aren't we?" I said.

Milton walked to the door and scanned the woods. "Well," he said, "I ain't sure that the elk killers and whoever did this ain't the same thing."

"If they are," I said, "then it's too big for us."

"Maybe you're right," Milton said. He took one last look around the cabin. "But then again, maybe you ain't."

"Either way, it's too late to do anything tonight," I said.

Milton looked off along the ridge, as if contemplating going farther.

"Yeah," he said, "I reckon you're right. I'll tell the rangers about it in the morning."

We walked to the horses, rode back down the mountainside, and followed the river back to Whitehead's Landing, neither of us saying much. The wind picked up. Traces of clouds drifted over the mouth of the canyon. The meth lab worried me. Elk killers, I could almost understand. It made sense that somebody who'd lost his land would take it out on those foreign elk, but this methamphetamine—I didn't know. I'd moved out here because of the serenity, the peace and quiet that comes with nature. Nothing was safe anymore.

After the patrol, I slept most of Sunday. It was almost dark by the time I'd gotten up and, in the cold, hauled in a rick of firewood for my wood stove. I stirred the coals in the stove and watched a half-burnt log reignite. I closed the door and opened the draft to let the log flame up good before adding a couple more logs and letting them catch.

I showered, banked the fire, closed down the draft on the stove, and left my house on Acropolis Road to go to Jessup for something to eat. Hanging around the house alone often made me feel uneasy and restless. An architect friend from college designed this house for my ex and me, but Patricia left me with the prints and no house. I decided to build it anyway, only out in the country rather than in that new development we'd picked along the North Fork of the White River, near Goshen. No use letting a nice design go to waste. I decided to build in Hayes County to be near the Bison River. When I was a kid, my father used to bring me over here before it was even a national river. We'd put a canoe in at the old low-water bridge at Baptismal and pay a local to drive our truck down to Hasty, waiting on us when we arrived. We'd float the river, fish the best pools, camp along the banks, and fry the fish we'd caught. As I grew into a teenager, the trips became less frequent. My father got a railroad job and had to work weekends. By the time I reached high school, two springs had passed since we'd last floated the Bison. I got my license to drive and began chasing girls. Then came college, marriage, two daughters, divorce, and finally a feeling that I'd lost something, that time had slipped me by. I moved here with hopes of finding what I'd lost and to slow time down.

But my new house was big, and it had Patricia's mark on it—the rooms she'd wanted, like a sitting room; a study; and a big master bath with a double vanity, refurbished claw-foot bathtub, and glass-block shower stall. Those spaces still seemed like hers even though she'd never set foot in the place, even though I'd hung gun and fishing-rod racks on the walls in them and put a pool table in her planned sitting room.

The rooms for my girls, Sarah and Rhiannon, were the hardest to deal with. I'd moved in beds and dressers designed for girls, but I hated to see them bring their things when they visited and take them all back home when they returned to their mother, leaving the dressers empty. Sometimes, I'd open the drawers, hoping to see a pair of pajamas or anything else left behind, to assure me they'd be back, despite, legally, knowing they would be. Still, when you're a divorced father with only once-a-month visiting privileges, you have a hard time feeling confident about your future with your kids.

Driving past the Bison River Tourist Court, I looked to see if the Saturn was still there. It was. The window of the cabin was yellow with light. I thought about stopping, inviting her to dinner, but I convinced myself she wasn't interested, that she was just passing through. I drove on. Along the short Main Street and around the courthouse square, Christmas decorations had been attached to the streetlight poles—alternating snowmen and candy canes. Frost was crystallizing on the windshields of the parked cars.

Inside the Ozark Inn, I saw her at a booth, by herself, smoking, reading a book. A coffee cup steamed near the book.

I walked over, said, "Boo."

She jumped slightly.

"One up on you again," I said.

"Paybacks are hell," she said, smiling at me. "Here alone?"

"Yep." Inferring an invitation, I sat down and glanced at the book. Its spine was creased until it was nearly unreadable, and the cover was missing. Three "Used" stickers from a college bookstore were on the first page, and someone, maybe she, had added "Conf" to one "Used" sticker, "Ab" to another, and "Mis" to the third. "What are you reading?" I asked.

"*The Great Gatsby*," she said and closed the book. "Found it in the indoor rummage sale. I read it in college, but everything else they had was murder mysteries, romances, or horror novels. I didn't care to read about any of that."

Pointing at the book, I said, "Well, you've got some murder, romance, and mystery in there."

"I suppose," she said. "But that's not the whole point of it."

I winked at her. "At least that's what the professors always told us." She smiled again, and I studied her a moment. "You come here to just read, or did you eat yet?"

"I ate," she said, "but I don't mind watching." She sipped coffee and took out another cigarette. "Mind if I smoke?"

Though I sort of did, I said, "Not at all," and grabbed a menu from behind the napkin dispenser. The waitress came, took my order, brought me coffee too.

I raised my cup to the woman across the booth from me and said, "Here's to chance meetings."

She clinked her cup against mine. "To chance meetings."

Her eyes were the green color of tarnished copper, her cheeks were a little hollow but delicate, she had almost imperceptible crow's-feet, and the skin under her chin was tight and smooth—she was aging with grace. I was glad to be sitting across from a woman who wasn't almost a generation younger than I was or who wasn't worn down by several kids and a no-good ex-husband.

We talked as I ate, mostly about me. I told her where I was from, why I moved here.

"Where's Fayetteville from here?" she asked and lit another cigarette.

"Didn't you come through there to get here?" I asked.

"I wasn't paying any attention," she said.

"It's an hour west of here," I said and told her I'd left my engineer's job at the city sewage-treatment plant. "Well, you've heard of crap jobs," I said.

"Yours was literal."

I took a sip of coffee, lowered my voice a notch. "And in the meantime, my ex-wife decided it wasn't very glamorous either."

"Was she a little uppity?"

"Not at first." I told her about Sarah and Rhiannon.

"Fleetwood Mac fans, huh?"

"Well, she was," I said. "I see the girls once a month out here. A friend of mine has horses he lets them ride. They like the country, at least one of them does."

"At least one of them takes after you, I guess."

Though I hoped she was right, I said, "Lord, I hope not." I figured women like humility. They're also intrigued by a mean streak.

"They could do worse, I imagine."

Over the loudspeakers, dogs barked "Jingle Bells." I looked at the mount of a twelve-point buck on the wall adjacent to us. A Santa's hat was on its head. Christmas bulbs dangled from the antlers. A red ball was stuck on its nose. Patricia would cringe, but Margot seemed to settle right in.

"So what's your ex do that's so prestigious?" she asked.

"Works for Wal-Mart."

Her eyebrows arched. "And she dumped you?"

I laughed. "Well, she's an MBA. Washington University in St. Louis, a rich kids' school. Works at Wal-Mart's corporate office in Bentonville. The higher up Wal-Mart's ladder she climbed, the less appealing me and my job looked. At least that's the idea I let eat away at me."

"Delusion," she said. "A breakup's best medicine."

"You don't sound like you're from Texas," I said.

She glanced away and swayed a little to a Muzak version of "White Christmas" that followed the barking dogs. "I grew up in Tennessee," she said, flicking ashes into the tray. "When I was in junior high school, my daddy moved us to Texas to find work."

I let her take a couple more drags and asked, "How long are you in town?"

"I don't know," she said. "Seemed like a good isolated place to get away from everything for a while."

"Everything?"

She finished off her coffee, took another drag from her cigarette. "It's a long story."

"The new car and all?"

"Yeah." She ground out the cigarette. "Well, Mr. Powell," she said, "I should get back to my little cabin even though I feel like I'm in solitary confinement in that thing."

I wanted to tell her I had a large three-bedroom house all to myself, but I took a business card from my wallet instead, handed it to her, something I didn't often do in nonbusiness situations. "Ever need anything," I said, "give me a call."

She took it, looked at it, slipped it into her purse. "I will," she said. She slid from the booth, put on her parka, tucked the book under her arm, and left. I ordered another cup of coffee and a slice of peach pie and wondered where the hell she came from and who she was. Being suspicious of her bothered me—we'd gotten along fine. No real awkwardness, even after the way we'd met. She was easy to talk to, easy to be with. Sharing a booth with someone isn't always easy.

On the way home, I looked at the yellow square of light in number five. A car horn blew in front of me. I jerked the wheel and whipped back onto my side of the double line. One thing about Jessup, there are no women. Sometimes, I'd go to Eureka Springs, an old turn-of-the-century resort town and the closest "wet" town. I liked to stay in the historic hotel rooms, drink in the old bars that were speakeasies in the '20s. A couple of times, I'd shared the experience with a companion, usually one of the hippie or New Age artists who lived in town and drank at the bars. Or when I went to Fayetteville to visit the girls, I'd get a room and go out after taking them home. I met an older grad student once, a city girl from the west coast who claimed to be a writer. I'd screwed up and gave her my card too. Afterward, she kept calling me, but I ignored her. She didn't understand those encounters were short-term, but Margot seemed more independent than that city girl and less likely to call me all the time.

The next day, Milton stopped by the tourist court as Harris and I unloaded a plastic shower stall from the back of my truck. The shower stalls sort of violated the authentic 1920s look of the cabins, but Mrs. Suddeth said customers are willing to compromise modern conveniences everywhere except in the bathroom.

Milton filled us in on his meeting with the rangers about the meth lab as we carried the stall inside the cabin.

"Meth labs?" Harris said. "Here?"

"Looks like it," I said.

Milton kept talking from the doorway as we set the stall on the bare bathroom floor and worked the unit into its framed alcove, which was finished with water-resistant wallboard. Most builders only ran the wallboard to just below the height of the shower stall and left the studs bare, but I took the wallboard all the way to the floor—better insulated, and it kept the bugs and the varmints out. And doing so only cost me about a sheet of wallboard per bathroom.

"Rangers are out searching the old barns and whatnot along the river for more," Milton said. "They got a Hazmat team cleaning up the one we found. And a bomb squad detonating booby-traps."

"Booby-traps?" I asked.

"Yep," Milton said. "Homemade landmines. If it ain't one sort of meanness, it's another." He looked at me. "You riding with me again Saturday night?"

"This does add a new element," I said, "but I'll still go along, I guess."

Milton nodded, looked at Harris. "You wanna come, Harris? Got plenty of horses. You could ride Rooster Cogburn."

"He got an eye patch?"

"No," Milton said, chuckling, "but I reckon I could get one if you wanted it."

"I'd better not," Harris said. "Old lady wouldn't like it much. She likes for me to watch the baby on weekends so her and her sisters can go to town."

"Well," Milton said, "you're welcome anytime."

"From what I heard about meth, the way it fucks people up, I don't know if I'd go down there anyways," Harris said. "Makes people hyper. Paranoid. Trigger happy."

"Really?" I said.

"You gonna chicken out on me now are you?" Milton asked me.

"No, but this—"

"We're just acting like eyes," he said. "We see something, we call the rangers." He stood there for a moment. "Well, I be seeing you," he said, maybe sensing I had some doubts and wanting to take off before I could change my mind. He climbed in his truck, started it, and pulled away. We waved at his dented and horseshit-stained tailgate, the wooden cattle racks rattling on the bed of the truck.

I *was* having doubts, even though I felt obligated to Milton. He was the first person around here who gave me a contracting job. Other folks seemed leery of me, but Milton came by my house, liked how it looked, and asked if I'd build him a screened-in porch on the back of his house. I knew he didn't need a porch, and if he really wanted one, he could've built it himself. He told me he didn't mind seeing a man like me move in, that he admired a man who tried to beat the daily grind and do what he wanted, like I'd done. He said if he could've gotten paid for riding horses instead of working, he'd have stopped riding only long enough to sleep.

When I finished the porch, Milton scrutinized it. The joints in the lumber were tight, plenty of nails, good-quality lumber, everything plumb and level. He decided for sure that I wasn't some jackleg. After that job, others started coming. I wasn't overrun with work, but I got all I needed.

Meanwhile, I waited on a chance to return the favor for him. That chance came last summer. The temperature was over a hundred every day for a couple of weeks, and Milton's damn turkeys were cooking alive, dying of heat prostration. Milton had hoped he could wait the heat wave out, but the weatherman had forecast at least another week of it. Milton called me up, asked if I'd help him get rid of some dead turkeys. Thinking he meant a few dozen or so, I said, "Okay. Sure."

At his house, Milton was waiting with a hundred boxes of shells and a couple of .22 magnum rifles. He handed me one of the guns and a box of shells and asked, "You know how to shoot that?"

"Well, yeah," I said, but I was confused. I thought the turkeys were already dead. "What are we shooting?"

"Follow me," he said. We headed toward his turkey barns, which stood at the head of a hollow that eventually led down to the Bison. We went to the first barn. Inside, at least half the turkeys were dead. Panting, eyes half-covered with blue lids, the rest were barely hanging on. Milton took his gun off safety and raised the stock to his shoulder. He sighted down on a turkey and fired. A poof of feathers and a bird fell. One of his horses out in the barn whinnied. "Jack Cutter," Milton said, staring at the dead bird. "Always been gun-shy." Milton looked at me, and then we both started shooting. An hour later, ears ringing, the air stinking of gunpowder, turkey shit, blood, and raw poultry, I staggered outside of the third barn to keep the stench from gagging me.

I noticed a turkey pecking around in the field. He'd escaped one of the barns while we were shooting. I raised my rifle, aiming at the bird. He appeared healthy. As I was about to pull the trigger, Milton said, "Hold it, Frank."

I glanced at him.

"I'll keep thatun. He looks like a survivor."

As we scooped up turkey carcasses with a front-end loader and dumped them in Milton's truck to haul to the landfill's incinerator, that turkey pecked around in the middle of the field. Milton kept him and treated him like a dog ever since, even feeds him dog food.

Later that afternoon, I saw Margot leave her room and get in her car. I wondered whether she was checking out. She had no luggage with her, and she didn't stop to drop off the key. She pulled out of the parking lot, headed west out of town.

"Nice looking lady, ain't she?" Harris asked.

I glanced at him. "Not bad at all."

"Why you suppose she's here?"

"I've been wondering that myself," I said. "She's hard to pin down."

"You tried, did you?"

I faked a right at him, gave him a finger punch in the gut with my left, and he mimed a combination and jabbed my right shoulder with a right cross a bit harder than I was expecting. I started to grab it but didn't want to let on that I'd felt the blow. He was grinning at me. "Let's get that commode inside," I said.

"Get your mind out of it first," he said. "Won't be so heavy thataway."

I'd hired Harris back in the summer, after I'd gone through three men who didn't know which end of the nail to hit or which end of the hammer to hit it with, but those were the only kind who'd risk working for a new contractor like me. Until Harris showed up. One day he just walked out of his job at the Tyson plant in Berryville. Couldn't take anymore. I couldn't blame him. I wouldn't wish forty hours or more a week of eviscerating chickens on anyone. Harris had been in Vietnam, unlike me. I came of age just barely after the draft was ended. He had a wife, his third, and a fifteen-month-old kid. He had four other kids from his other two marriages. After telling me about his arrest, Harris said he'd been clean ever since. I believed him because he worked hard.

Before I left work that evening, and after not seeing Margot come back, I stopped by the tourist-court office. Mrs. Suddeth said she hadn't checked out. Her things were still in her room when they'd cleaned it. "Do you know her?" she asked.

"I'm getting there," I said.

At home, after a shower and a frozen pizza, I'd almost called her room several times but didn't. I convinced myself she wasn't back yet or that she'd returned and left. She was no more attractive than anyone else I'd dated, or married, but she wore mystery the way some women wear exactly the right kind and right amount of fragrance. I liked her easygoing manner, just enough refinement, just enough of a raw edge, but I was still nervous. Even when something seems like fate, you can't help but doubt yourself, to think you're making something out of nothing.

I started to call again, but the plate, fork, and beer glass I'd just dirtied needed cleaning. I sat them in the sink, turned on the faucet, and the phone rang. I shut the water off, answered it.

"Is this Powell's Construction and Remodeling?"

It was her, her voice trying to feign business. Sweat moistened my hand that gripped the receiver. "Yes, ma'am, it is," I said, playing along.

"What's your reputation, I mean, as a remodeler?"

"I do the best work around. Ask anybody."

"Can you make a sober lady drunk?" she asked, sounding more country than she had before. "'Cause, honey, there ain't a drink to be found in this town."

"It's dry as kilned wood," I said. "But I'm not. Got a fifth of Maker's Mark with the wax still unbroken."

"Sounds like you're the man for the job."

I switched the receiver to my other hand, wiped my right palm on the leg of my pants. With a technical pencil, I started tracing her name over and over on my message pad. "I'll be right there."

"I'd rather come there," she said. "Too cramped here. I'm going stir crazy."

"We can fix that too. I got all the room you need."

"I need all I can get."

I gave her directions, changed shirts three times until I found one—a sky-blue Oxford—that was less wrinkled than the others. I swabbed a couple of highball glasses to clean off the dishwasher spots and the dust. The matching highball, beer, wine, and champagne glasses in the liquor cabinet were Patricia's idea. She liked to host dinner parties for her Wal-Mart cronies, but she left me with the glasses. Why, I don't know. I normally drink from whatever glasses are handy. Until now, those glasses in the cabinet hadn't been touched since I'd put them there when I moved in.

Patricia and I came from two different worlds. My family owned a farm west of Fayetteville, near Lincoln. And my dad was a signal maintainer for the Arkansas/Missouri Railroad, a small line that runs from Joplin to Fort Smith. My mom had never had a job outside the house. My family had always made out fine, but they kept things simple. Meals were necessary parts of the day, like feeding the cattle or weeding the garden.

Patricia's family, though, was not quite the same. Her folks were both professionals in St. Louis. They had cocktails before dinner. They used salad bowls instead of putting salad on the dinner plate. They laid their butter knives across the edge of small bread plates that held rolls or slices of French bread. They set out a water glass and another glass for wine, ice tea, or whatever. They used napkins, not paper towels, and they laid them across their laps.

Margot's car turning into the driveway sent my dogs to barking. From the front door, I called them away, sent them around back. Wearing a long, brown, wool coat, not the parka, she climbed out of her car. Her hair was different, darker, flatter, straighter, but not much shorter. I preferred this style. Below the hem of her coat were thin ankles covered with dark leggings. She wore leather shoes appropriate for winter. If I'd gotten only a glimpse of her on the street, especially from behind, I didn't know that I'd have recognized her. I held the door open and she walked inside, a light fragrance of tea rose following her in.

I took her coat. She had on a knee-length, black, floral-print dress, the neckline plunging to her shoulder blades in the back. On her pale skin was fine peach fuzz, and I wanted to glide the tips of my fingers over it. I told her to have a seat and hung her coat in the foyer closet.

"Nice place," she said, looking around. "I like the cathedral ceiling. The wood. It feels warm."

"Thanks," I said. "An architect friend I went to school with designed it." Hands clasped behind her back, she examined the living room. "No Christmas tree?"

"Haven't been feeling too Christmassy."

"Stone hearth. Wood stove. No fireplace? You can't hang stockings above a wood stove."

"Stove's more efficient," I said. "If I'm gonna cut and split wood, I want heat from it. Santa'll have to use the front door."

"A bit of a Scrooge, aren't you?"

"Disappointed?"

"Well," she said, "seems to me bourbon and fireplaces do go hand in hand."

"One out of two's not bad." She smiled. "No, I guess not."

I asked her how she liked her bourbon.

"On the rocks with just a kiss of club soda."

I liked the way she said *kiss*, as if it were a two-syllable word.

She picked up a picture of Rhiannon and Sarah from the coffee table. "Pretty girls," she said.

"Thanks," I said. "They must've got their looks from their mother."

She set the picture down. "Modesty will get you everywhere," she said and took a seat on the couch.

I mixed the drink, handed it to her. She downed it in one gulp, gave the glass back to me before I could even turn to go to my chair. Impressed, I examined the glass a moment. She drank like someone who needed to.

As I mixed another, I said, "Nice dress."

"Thanks. Went shopping today," she said. "I have very few things with me. Found an outlet mall in Branson." She fluffed the hem of her dress. "Got a couple of good deals."

"First time to Branson?"

"Yes. God." She laughed. "It's a little gaudy. Never seen so much neon before."

"It's all fancy facades on cheap metal buildings. It's the only concept we understand," I said, carrying the drink to her. "Make everything look like a TV—a dolled-up front and three blank sides."

"A bit cynical, aren't you?"

I shrugged. "When you take pride in building things, you hate to see people build crap and make a lot of money for it." I handed her the drink and sat down. "You probably lowered the average age in Branson by twenty years."

"It was actually a little dead," she said. "And there was no place open that served drinks." She took a sip, set the glass on a coaster on the coffee table. The coasters were hard leather and had the American Society of Civil Engineers insignia on them. Patricia had gotten them for me when I passed the preliminary E.I.T. exam to get my civil engineer's license. I still hadn't taken the final exam.

"So, why are you here?" I asked.

"Your house?"

I laughed. "Well, yeah, and in Jessup, of all places." She set her glass on the coffee table. "It does make me wonder—an attractive woman, new car. You just show up here."

She took out a cigarette, nodded at it. "All right?" I got an ashtray from the bar, placed it beside her empty glass, and sat back down. She lit the cigarette and said, "My husband was killed recently."

"How?" I asked, now afraid she'd be too distraught and heartbroken to be interested in me. Then I felt selfish for thinking that way.

"Armed robbery on our back porch."

"Were you there?"

She glanced at me, her eyes watering a little, her hands trembling. "Look, I'd rather not talk about it." She downed the drink.

I studied her for a few seconds and grabbed her glass. "Another?" She nodded, took another drag from her cigarette, and wedged it in a crenel in the ashtray. As I mixed the drinks, I noticed her dabbing her eyes with a Kleenex. "You okay?" I asked, handing her the drink.

"Yeah," she said, "but let's talk about you."

I nodded and sat down beside her. "Alright. What do you wanna know?"

"Why'd you really pick construction over engineering?"

"Well, for one," I said, "I wanted to avoid the middleman when I built my house—and I wanted to build my own house." I looked around the room, admiring the stained wood in the cathedral ceiling, the tight seams in the V-notches. "After my divorce, I felt like I was putting myself back together by building this house. And when I got involved with it and hired a couple of guys to help, I found myself absorbed in it." I stopped and noticed she was looking around the house again. "Am I boring you?"

"No," she said, crossing her hands in her lap. "I like listening to you talk about things you like. I like imagining you building this."

"Well, we took our time and built it right. We paid attention to details in this framing this world hasn't seen in fifty years or better. Building this house was a learning process for me. In more ways than one."

"How so?"

"Well, I learned I could do it. And I learned I could get over something like a divorce. I found some independence, but I also learned about the loneliness that can come with it."

"You don't have to be alone to be lonely," she said.

"Nope. I was lonelier when I was making more money and working a job I hated." I looked at her and laughed. "Now I'm poorer but happier," I said, "if you can believe that."

"Well," she said. "I know about poor but not so much about happy."

"You don't look poor."

She crossed her legs and again smoothed out her dress. "I *was* growing up, and I knew the only way out was college," she said. "I made good grades, got a scholarship, went to college, and became a teacher at a small high school. Then the state consolidated all the rural high schools in my county, and I was out of a job."

"Then what?"

She looked at me, leaning toward me a little closer, I thought, if only just a few fractions of an inch. "I met my husband, he died, and I ended up here."

"That leaves a lot of gaps between meeting your husband and ending up here."

"The last part's the important part," she said, obviously leaning toward me now. "Right?"

Still holding my drink in my left hand, I placed my right hand under her chin and kissed her. Her lips were soft and moist and tasted of bourbon and faintly of cigarettes. Her eyes closed and her mouth opened a little. As I started to really kiss her, she pulled away.

"This is a little fast," she said. She finished off the drink and stood. Carrying her glass to the bar, she stopped near the phone. She studied my notepad, where I'd written her name. She picked it up. Now I was nervous about having traced the letters of her name over and over. Maybe she'd think I was an obsessive psychopath or something, but she stared at the pad with an odd sadness in her eyes and ran the tips of her fingers along the letters as if committing a strange new language to memory. Her unpolished nails were as clear as my desire for her. She glanced at her watch and said, "I should be going."

"But—"

"It's okay," she said. "It's okay. It's just me. I had a nice time."

She smiled, and I got her coat.

"Are you okay to drive?" I asked. "The road's steep down off this mountain."

"I've driven worse," she said. I helped her into her coat, and she stepped outside, stopped, and turned around. She looked at me and looked at the porch floor. "Listen, I'm okay," she said. "Thanks for the drinks."

From the front porch, I watched her climb in her car and disappear down Acropolis Road. I listened until the sound of her car was swallowed up by the silent, frosty darkness. I stood there a short while longer. The dogs came around the house and sat down at my feet. Still watching the road, I scratched one behind the ears. Then I went back inside, out of the cold.

The next day at the job site, I caught a glimpse of Harris's eyes, red and half-lidded, bags underneath. His face had at least a three-day growth, not that being clean-shaven was a requirement for the construction industry. Hanging from under his Razorbacks cap, his peppery-colored hair was greasy and stringy. "You look like you either had way too good a time last night or you've been through hell, one," I said.

"Baby was up all night, third goddamn night in a row," he said. "The croup."

"Wanna go home and rest?"

"Yeah, to tell the truth," he said, "but I reckon I can make it till lunch. We'll have those kitchen fixtures plumbed by then anyways."

"Sounds alright to me," I said. "We can put down the linoleum in there tomorrow, then get started on the tiles. I'd like to have the cabin painted and papered by Sunday."

As we were unloading linoleum from my truck, two state police cruisers pulled into the parking lot, their cars clean and glinting in the morning sunlight. Four troopers went to the office. A minute or so later, Mrs. Suddeth led them out. For a moment I feared she was taking them to Margot's cabin, but she led them to the bow hunters' cabin instead and opened the door.

"What do they want?" Harris asked, staring at them.

"Looks like those guys from Missouri," I said. "Wonder if they have anything to do with the elk."

"Ain't seen that Bronco of theirs for two days," he said. "Figured they was gone."

I glanced at Margot's cabin, saw her peeking through a narrow part between the curtains in the window. She tugged them back together.

Harris and I walked to the bow hunters' cabin. Mrs. Suddeth said, "Their families called those two fellers in missing."

Wearing surgical gloves, the troopers carried out a couple of suitcases, plastic bags filled with papers, pencils, bottles of buck lure, arrowheads, pocketknives, beer cans, and convenience-store sandwich wrappers. "You been working here all week?" one of the troopers asked us.

"All fall," Harris said.

"When was the last time you saw a green Bronco here?"

"Must've been two days ago," I said. "We figured they'd left for good."

"Anyone else been here this week?"

"In number five," I said. "Don't think she knows any more than we do, though."

"Guess I'll find out," he said and headed in Margot's direction. He knocked a couple of times before she answered. They talked for a few minutes. She shook her head, shrugged her shoulders, and he headed back toward the other troopers.

I got my nerve up and went to Margot's cabin, knocked on the door. It eased open, the chain refastened and stretched taut. "Afternoon," I said.

"Hi." She watched me for a couple of seconds.

"You keep that door chained shut," I said, "and I might start believing I made all the wrong moves last night."

"Sorry." She fumbled with the chain before getting it unfastened, and I stepped inside. She stared outside a moment longer and closed the door behind me.

"You all right?" I asked.

"Yes. Fine."

The room was dark but warm. Flames in a couple of lead-glass candleholders flickered on the dining table, and the air smelled like vanilla. She'd done a little decorating, I was glad to see. On the counter near the TV was a picture of an elderly woman. I picked it up and studied it. She looked a little like Margot.

"That's my mother," Margot said. "The only bad part about getting away from it all is missing her."

"She doesn't know where you are?"

"She knows," she said. "But that doesn't make her any closer."

I nodded. We stood there in an awkward silence. Finally, I asked, "What if I showed you something beautiful this afternoon?"

She smiled for the first time that morning. "How can a girl turn something beautiful down?"

"Good question," I said. "Three o'clock?"

"You know where to find me."

I returned her smile, nodded, and left. Outside, the troopers taped the hunters' cabin off with yellow police tape. As I approached number four, Harris was waiting on me. "Got a date?" he asked, grinning again.

"Yep," I said. "Think I'll take her down to Whitehead Creek, show her the elk while there are still some left."

"That orta make her swoon," he said, rolling his bloodshot eyes.

"Of course elk-watching requires a bottle or two of wine and a picnic basket."

"Wine? Picnic baskets?" he said. "Jesus."

"Women like that shit," I said, but what I didn't say was that I did too.

"Till you marry them," he said. "Then they like money and babies. I know, I been through three now, and all they wanted was money and babies. Same old shit, man."

I wasn't used to that kind of anger in Harris's voice, but I figured he was just a little stressed out. I knew for sure then that giving him the rest of the day off was a good idea. Tomorrow he'd be good as new.

"It's beautiful," Margot said, gazing up at the gray cliffs across the narrow river. The valley was wide here, at Whitehead Creek, where the tiny stream dumped into the Bison. Here were campgrounds, horse barns, a canoe launch. In an old ranch-style stone house, taken over by the government after the land was bought, was the rangers' station.

We were parked at the canoe launch. This was the time of year when the dry season gives way to the wet. The water was low and clear, but that would change soon, and the river would become swift and greenish and would scour away the skin of leaves that lined the stream bottom in the slack water.

"God sure knew what He was doing when He created this," she said.

"See those lines etched in the limestone wall?" I said, pointing at the cliffs. The rock face is mostly smooth, except for the horizontal lines every few feet. You can mark significant changes in the water level over the centuries much like you can count the rings of a tree to figure its age. As an engineer, I learned just enough about the physics of nature to not believe in creation.

"Yes," she said.

"The river's done that over time, always eroding this canyon," I said. "Would it be fair to give God all the credit for the river's work?"

"Well," she said, "like Adam and Eve, a river's been given free rein to make its own way." She gazed downstream, where the river bent against another high rock face on our side and disappeared behind a sandstone gravel bar.

"Is that what you're doing now?" I asked. "Making your own way?"

"I suppose it is," she said. "And it's about as hard as wearing down that rock." She scanned the fields behind me and glanced at me. "Now where are those elk you've talked so much about?"

We drove out of Whitehead Creek and headed toward Baptismal, crossed the bridge over the river, and parked beneath it. Fields lay to the south of the road, and nine elk, scattered about, grazed in the closest field. Standing near the tree line along the back of the field, near the river, a large bull bugled.

"Wow," Margot said. "I've heard that on TV, but it sounds really strange in person."

"The females seem to like it."

"Give me flowers any day," she said.

"How about wine instead?"

"Or wine."

We eased into the edge of the field, spread out a blanket, unpacked the basket, uncorked the wine, and filled two glasses. "To the mountains," I said, and we toasted.

After she sipped the wine, she watched a couple of young bulls sparring near an uninterested cow. The clacking of their interlocked antlers echoed along the river. A car passed on the bridge, slowing so the driver could look at the elk. A few people had gathered at the split-rail fence a little farther down the road to watch and take photos. Then she gazed at the ridges around us. "Reminds me so much of home," she said.

"Tennessee?"

She nodded. "Definitely not Fort Worth."

As we ate my attempts at gourmet sandwiches, I watched her slow, careful observations of the river valley. She took it in a little at a time, as if committing it to memory. The dread that she might not be long for the area rose in me. "What are you running from, Margot?"

"Do you really wanna know?"

"Well, to tell you the truth, I can't stop thinking about it."

"Neither can I." She stared into her glass of wine for more than a minute, and then she glanced at me and took another sip. She lit a cigarette and watched the elk. "My husband and I were robbed coming in the back door of the house from the garage." Still not looking at me, she paused, took a drag from her cigarette, blew smoke. "The garage was detached from the house," she said. "Funny, the designer said it was safer that way."

She finished off her wine and chose words like a good framer chooses a wall stud, eyeing for straightness and trueness. "They came from the alley behind the garage, two of them," she said. "They had Halloween masks on, two of the Seven Dwarfs, Sneezy and Grumpy. That struck me as so strange I forgot what was going on for a moment, until they demanded Arnold's wallet, my purse, our jewelry. But Arnold was always easy to rile. He was a loudmouth too, liked to argue. One of the things I liked about him was he hated to lose an argument." She looked at me. "That bottle run dry, or does this place have a three-drink maximum?"

I poured more wine, glad she was talking, whether her story was true or not. She sipped from her glass, rested it on her thigh, her legs crossed. "Where was I?"

"The robbers," I said, still on my first glass of wine.

"They demanded our things," she said. "Arnold told them to fuck off." She paused, took another sip, swallowed hard. "One of the men shot him. It was so loud. I stood there, staring at the second man, my husband writhing on the ground for a few moments before he died. The second man pointed his gun at me. I begged him not to kill me.

"The first man rifled Arnold's pockets, stripped off his Rolex, his wedding band, tie clip. Anything hard and shiny, they took it. Then he took my jewelry, my purse, yanked the earrings from my lobes, and told me to lie down. The earrings left scars."

"I noticed that," I said. "That must've hurt."

"I didn't feel it." She sipped again. "I lay down on the brick patio, crying because I knew I was going to die beside a man I didn't love, and everyone would think that we'd died together. Some romantic b.s. like that. I was only there because I didn't have the guts to leave him. After I lost my job, I guess maybe I panicked." She stopped talking, downed the rest of the wine, and held her glass out to me. I finished mine and refilled both glasses. She lit another cigarette and smoked it furiously.

"Did they catch the men?"

"No," she said and killed that glass. "Not yet."

"Wouldn't it look bad for you to leave town?"

"Everyone thinks I'm visiting an aunt in Memphis," she said. "And I called her and told her where I was. I told her that I had to get away for a while. They can find me if they need to." Holding the cigarette between her lips, she pulled the other bottle of wine from the basket. She grabbed the corkscrew and carefully twisted it into the cork, held the bottle between her knees, and pulled the cork out until it popped. "But I did have to get away," she said. "Everything around me held the death of Arnold. Even the clothes in my closet, and I couldn't take it." She took one last drag from the cigarette and stubbed it out on the ground.

"It wasn't your fault they—"

"It was my fault he believed I loved him," she snapped. She averted her eyes and fiddled with the pack for another cigarette, her fingers shook. A couple of more cigarettes came out with the one she pinched, falling onto the blanket.

"You don't have to talk," I said and grabbed the bottle, filling her glass again.

"Well," she said, trying to place the two cigarettes back into the pack. "After getting it off my chest, it doesn't seem so bad."

"Your husband's death?"

"No," she said. "Talking about it." She focused on me for several moments before looking out across the field as she sipped the wine. "Murder's nothing like you expect. I mean, not like what you've always seen on TV or in the movies. In real life, it's fast and loud. And there's this silence that follows right after the gunshot, like the volume of the whole world has been turned down. There's this emptiness. I cried until I drained myself."

"Because he was shot?"

"Because I wasn't." She drank again and gazed off at the elk. Crows cawed from the woods across the river. Overhead, a jet's twin contrails were growing ragged. Two elk started sparring, the antlers clacking and knocking against each other. Finally, the larger of the elk got leverage, locked the other's antlers in his, lowered his head, and drove the smaller elk backwards for about ten yards. The smaller elk shook loose and trotted toward the woods at the back of the field. Shaking his head and stamping his hooves, the larger elk watched from the middle of the field.

"Let's go," Margot said, glaring at the triumphant elk.

Back at my house, I stoked the fire in the stove. There was still some Maker's Mark left over from her last visit, so I mixed a couple of drinks, sat on the couch next to her. "You know, Margot," I said, "meeting you almost makes me wanna believe in fate."

"What I believe is this," she said. "I believe I'd like you to sit a little closer." Her voice was like music. I scooted closer, set my drink on the coffee table. I started to say more, but she said, "Shhh," and placed her fingers against my lips. I took her arm by the wrist and lowered her hand to the cushion. I leaned my face into hers, and we kissed. A short one at first and then longer. That rose fragrance. With my arm around her, holding her tightly, she felt like she should always be there. Her hand came to rest on my cheek. After we kissed, she stood and took my hand to help me from the couch. For the first time, I thought she might stay—because of me. I rose to my feet and she led me into my bedroom.

The next morning, I dressed for work, leaving her lying in bed, a crazy quilt draped over her. She was the first woman since Patricia to still be in my bed the next morning. I kissed Margot's forehead, watched her stir a little, and wanted to stay there with her. But I knew I had to work, had to face Harris, and he'd tell by the look in my eye what had happened. A whole day of ribbing was in store for me, but I didn't much mind. I left her a note on the dresser saying I'd be back at lunch.

Harris was already working in number four, cementing tile to the bathroom walls, when I got there. He glanced at me and concentrated on his work. "Have a good time?"

"Yeah," I said, "but excuse me if I don't reveal the details."

"Every man's got a private side," he said, "and it ought to stay that way."

Digging for a trowel in the toolbox, I watched him from the corner of my eye. "A damn good philosophy."

A little after noon, Margot's car was gone when I pulled into the driveway. I went inside, looked for a note. I found mine, on the kitchen counter, with no reply. The bed hadn't been made, but she'd showered. An extra towel was wet. She hadn't returned to her cabin, at least not while I was there.

Ten minutes later, back at the tourist court, Harris was still at lunch. I asked Mrs. Suddeth if Margot had checked out.

"Not long after you left," she said.

"See which way she went?"

"Turned left out of here." Which meant she either went up Route 74 past my place or up Route 7 toward Harrison. If she were trying to elude me, she wouldn't take 74. I took 7 toward Harrison, knowing she had a good fifteen minutes on me. Hopefully the twisting road would slow her enough to allow me to catch up. Once she got to Harrison, there were any number of directions she could go. And she'd left no hint about where she might go next, except maybe east Tennessee.

Two miles out of Jessup, I overtook a Tyson's truck hauling chickens, going every bit of twenty-five. Feathers snowed down on me, and in the rearview, chicken-feather devils twisted in the wake of my truck. Veering in and out of the left lane whenever the striped lines marked a passing zone, I followed him for five miles before I could pass, cussing out loud. Within another mile, I was behind a kindergarten bus, stopping every fifty or so yards, it seemed, the stop sign flapping out from the side of the bus.

The trip to Harrison took forty-five minutes. From there, I traveled 65 north to the Missouri line, but saw no sign of her. I pulled over to the side of the road and sat there a few minutes, watching the road as if her car might appear over the rise. I gazed at the road for a while longer before turning around.

After work, I drove home, hoping her car would be there, but the driveway was empty, except for the dogs stretched out across the asphalt, catching the last of the sun.

Inside, my answering machine was silent, no beep and flashing red light holding the promise of her voice. I went to the bathroom, lifted the towel from the bar. It had mostly dried, except for dampness where it had been folded over the bar. I held it to my cheek, the last remnant of her presence cool and drying in the terry of the towel.

For a while I sipped the rest of the Maker's Mark, my fingers rotating the glass. The phone rang. So focused on Margot's absence, I barely heard the first ring. Then my brain kicked in. I slammed the glass on the end table, scrambled from the couch, grabbed the receiver just after the second ring, and said hello.

"Frank?" she said.

"Where are you?" I asked.

"Frank, I was going to call you to just thank you for being so kind," she said, "but I can't stop thinking about you. I . . . I can't think about what to do next without being distracted by you."

"Where are you?"

"Springfield," she said. "It was as far as I could get. I've been sitting in a restaurant for three hours trying not to call you."

"Come back," I said. "Please. Come back."

There was a pause. I could hear dishes clanking, people talking.

"Frank, I can't give enough back," she almost whispered. "I'm just not ready."

"I'll take whatever you have," I said.

"Frank," she said. Another pause. Canned Christmas music played in the background.

"What is it, Margot?"

"Frank, I'm on my way." She hung up.

The next two hours were excruciating. Every so often I'd want to take off for Springfield, in case she was lying. But why would she lie? And if she did, what good would it do for me to go after her? Lying would prove she didn't want to come back. But then why would she call?

Pacing, I listened for the dogs to announce her arrival, for the drone of her motor, for the whine of her tires on the road. Then I stood at the window and watched for her. Occasionally, a pair of headlights came down Acropolis Road, and I rushed to the front door, flung it open, waiting for Margot to pull into the drive. After the car passed, I closed the door back and paced again.

Finally, her lights swung from the road into my living room window, the dogs barking. I opened the front door, sent them to the back yard. She climbed from her Saturn and crept toward me. I was hoping for a mad dash, a collision of embraces, but I waited and watched. She stopped at the bottom of the three steps to the front porch. "I'm tired of running, Frank," she said, nearly crying.

"Come in," I said. "Come on into my house."

That Saturday night, Milton and I rode along the top of the bluffs instead of along the river. These trails were for hikers only, but we decided to alter our course to get a better perspective. We were approaching the Boy Scout camp when he said, "They found them two hunters today."

"They okay?"

"Dead. Both of them," he said. "Found them down near Hasty, but they'd been moved there from somewheres else."

"Something to do with the meth labs?" I asked.

"Looks like it. Them hunters stumbled up on one probably."

"Jesus."

He stopped Cahill. I pulled up alongside him. "They don't want us doing the patrols no more," he said.

"Who?"

"Them rangers."

"Now's a good time to tell me," I said.

"They think it's too risky for us."

"Well, they might be right."

"Hell, I don't care about no meth labs," he said. "I'm worried about the elk. Now them rangers are gonna be so focused on finding labs the elk are gonna be even more vulnerable."

"Might be true," I said. "But I don't mind admitting I'd rather be home right now."

He spurred Cahill back into motion. "Got that stranger lady staying with you now?"

Riding behind him, I looked at his back bobbing in the saddle in the quarter-moon light. "How'd you know?"

"Small town, Frank," he said. "They said she moved out of the cabin on Thursday."

"Wasn't like she had much to move."

"What's she hiding from? A jealous husband?"

"Don't know," I said, not wanting to tell her story, "but I'm glad she's hiding with me."

"You a lucky man," he said. "Have a woman just show up like that out here in the middle of nowhere. Ever wonder why?"

"Well, yeah," I said, "but you've heard that old saying about gift horses."

"There's also one about too good to be true." I slowed my horse and watched him for a few moments before catching up.

Another mile or so up the trail, Milton halted his horse and said, "Listen."

I stopped, steadied Jack Cutter. We stared down into the gorge. Around the bend, a motorcycle droned down the trail along the river, came around a curve, and crossed the river to the other side. Its light probed the woods, jerking from the rough trail. Where the canyon widened, the bike veered into a field overgrown with cedars, its taillight disappearing and reappearing. It climbed the gorge on the other side. A few seconds later, there was a flash, like a polaroid being taken, and then the sound of a muffled explosion, like a shotgun blast into a pillow.

Our horses recoiled. "Easy, Cahill," Milton said, reaching for Jack Cutter's bridle to calm him too.

We listened for several more moments. The bike was still idling. Milton started off. Thinking about those two hunters from Missouri, I let him go a few yards. "Milton," I said, "maybe we should just go to the rangers."

"Come on," he said, turning Cahill toward me. "If it's a meth lab, they gonna get out quick as they can."

"Then who's the guy on the bike?"

"Liable to be our elk killer." He turned, kicked Cahill into a trot. We eased down the steep slope to the river, where it bent, where the motorcycle had forded it. We hit the trail at a trot, knowing the path was clear of low-hanging tree limbs. We estimated where the motorcycle had turned into the field and listened for the idling bike. It had stalled out, but a voice was yelling for help. We followed it.

The man had dragged himself along a large, moss-covered log. He looked at us, eyes wild in Milton's flashlight beam. We dismounted, tied the horses off, and started toward him. He wore camouflaged coveralls, the front torn and slick with blood. He looked to be a little older than I was. "Don't kill me," he said, struggling to get the words out.

"It's alright," Milton said. "We gonna get you on out of here."

I shone my light on his motorcycle. It lay on the logging road, about thirty yards away. On the other side of the road was an old, leaning barn. I shined the light on the bike to get a better look, and I smelled the remains of a meth lab that had been in that barn. The front wheel of the bike had been shot through and crippled. Lying next to the bike was his weapon. "He's got a crossbow," I said.

"Get me that first-aid kit out of my saddlebag," Milton said. "We're gonna need to patch him up a little."

I went to the horses. As I dug through Milton's bag for the kit, I heard the zipper of the poacher's coveralls come down. Milton said, "Christ O'Mighty," stood, and lumbered toward me. He leaned against the tree the horses were tied to, shook his head, and said, "Never mind the first-aid kit."

I buckled the bag shut and crept toward the man, my light on him. Glistening intestines hung from a gash in his gut. He held his hand over it, and I could make out a wedding band on his bloody finger. "I can't feel my legs," he said. He was sobbing now, face slick with muddy sweat. He rolled his eyes up at me, their whites exaggerated.

"What're we gonna do, Milton?" I asked.

"He'll never make it out of here. I'll radio the rangers, tell them what's happened. You go down and wait for them by the trail. I'll stay here and keep the possums and coyotes away from him."

When I clicked off my light, the man dissolved into the darkness along the ground. Milton dug his walkie-talkie from the other saddlebag and radioed the rangers. I stood there for several moments, thinking about what Margot had said about the silence following her husband's death. I listened for it. I heard a low roar in my ears, and my stomach burned. I staggered off and vomited bile. The woods wheeled in the periphery of my vision. I tried to blink them static. For a few minutes I stood in the darkness and listened to the river in the distance, the only sound now in the canyon. A mist was rising from the water, and straight above me, in the mouth of the hollow, I could see a narrow band of star-pocked sky, all that was available to see. I felt closed in and alone, and I wanted nothing more than to be with Margot, than to have been with her all night and not have my own dead-body story now to tell her.

"You okay?" Milton asked.

"Yeah." I nodded and climbed on Jack Cutter.

I got home after daylight. Margot was up, sitting at the kitchen table, sipping coffee, waiting for me. The sections of the Sunday *Democrat-Gazette* were scattered before her. "I barely slept," she said.

"Sorry," I said. "Long night."

She watched as I leaned against the refrigerator, crossed my arms, and glanced at the floor. She knew something was wrong. "Frank, what happened out there?"

I went to the coffee maker, poured a cup, sat down at the table across from her, and told her about the guy on the motorcycle, the landmine, his stomach.

When I was done, she stood and moved to the sink to rinse her coffee cup out.

"He was dead by the time I got back with the rangers," I said. "They carted him out with a four-wheeler and a trailer. We followed. Milton didn't say a damn word the whole way back."

She leaned against the counter, facing me. "You okay?"

I nodded and sipped the coffee and swallowed.

For a while, we didn't talk, until she sat down across from me again and said, "I'm sorry, Frank."

"It's not your fault."

We stared at each other for nearly a minute before I glanced at the newspaper. The left column on the front page was reserved for anecdotes about bizarre crimes, inept criminals, and the like. There was a brief story about a man being caught in Asheville, North Carolina, after bragging in a bar to an off-duty cop about his connection to a murder/robbery in Triple Oaks, West Virginia. A couple returning home from dinner was robbed as they entered their house. The husband was shot, the wife escaped. Her name was Helen Spangler. The man claimed she'd hired him to kill the husband.

"You see this?" I asked Margot.

"What?" she said. I slid the paper to her, pointed at the story. "Sounds kind of like your story."

"I saw it," she said, staring off through the kitchen window. "Except mine happened in Texas." She squeezed a napkin in her fist. I followed her gaze and saw a deer nibbling brown grass at the other edge of the field behind the house. It glanced around, surveying the field for predators that had long since disappeared from these hills. The deer flicked its tail and lowered its head again to eat.

Finally, I stood, poured myself the last cup of coffee, and made a new pot. In the living room, I stoked the stove, and we sat on the couch, Margot leaning into me, her legs folded under her on the cushions. The coffee maker finished brewing in the kitchen, and the wind picked up outside. Through the windows I could see the trees scratching at the sky.

"I've brought this killing with me," she said. I put my arm around her, and she snuggled against me as closely as she could. For a long time, we sat quietly before the warm wood stove. We stared at the orange flickers in the vent holes along the bottom of the door. Outside, a gust of wind nudged the house, and the walls popped and cracked slightly. No matter how well you build a house, it's still at the mercy of nature. The wind blew again and the stove sucked air, drawing more flame from the logs. Occasionally the fire crackled and orange sparks shot from the vent, scattering across the clay hearth before fading to gray and black.

After supper, Milton dropped by, and I was glad to see him. I'd been worried about how he would take the death of that man in the woods.

He took his coat off, and I hung it up and led him into the living room, where I introduced him to Margot.

"Good finally meeting you, Margot," he said.

"I'm really sorry about last night," she said as I made drinks.

"Nothing that could of been done," Milton said, sitting in the straight-back rocker. "Except put a stop to those meth labs."

I gave him a drink and sat beside Margot on the couch. Watching Milton, she slid closer to me. I took a sip of bourbon and stared at the stove. Heat waves emanated from the cast iron, muddling the wall behind it.

"Jesus," Milton said. "This close to Christmas."

"Who was he?" I asked.

"Cody Lambert," Milton said. "From over near Low Gap. His family owned a bunch of that land down around Whitehead Creek. He went to Vietnam and then served another stint after the war. Came back and found out his family's farm went from eight hundred and some-odd acres to barely sixty. They got a fair price, like everybody else, but I don't guess you can put a price on a family's heritage."

"Took him long enough to act," I said.

"He waited till his old man died," Milton said. "'Least that's what I figured. Gar Lambert died of cancer not long before we started finding the elk dead, then Cody went to work on the elk."

"Why?" Margot asked.

"Hell, who knows? Word had it he came back from the army all messed up. Never could hold down a job. Separated. He'd lived in some halfway house down in Fort Smith off and on." Milton took another sip. "I knowed his daddy. He never liked me much after I came out in support of turning the river into a national park."

"Nobody likes losing his land."

"Well," Milton said, "we all lose things we don't wanna lose."

"But that man lost his life," Margot said.

Milton eyed her a moment and glanced away. "Rangers found a dozen more booby-traps today."

"God," Margot said. I glanced at her. She stared at the stove.

"Well, at least we found our elk killer," Milton said, shaking his head. "I expected different from our showdown with our poacher."

"Like what?" I asked.

"Hell, I don't know. I saw us apprehending him, having the pleasure of taking him in."

"It can't all be John Wayne," I said.

"Nope," he said. "I reckon not."

When we finished that round of drinks, I offered to make another, but Milton said no; he had to go soon, but he had something he wanted to show me. He went to his coat and pulled out a drafting compass and a USGS map and unfolded the map on the kitchen table. Margot and I studied the map. I showed her where we'd picnicked to give her some perspective. The upper third of the river snaked across the page. Contours showed the steepness of the bluffs, the gradual slope of the valley floor opposite them. Highlighted in yellow marker were seven buildings. Other buildings were shown, some near the water and others up on the mountainsides, but they had not been marked.

"Them marked houses are the ones rangers have found meth labs in," he said.

There appeared to be no particular pattern to their being used, except that none of the buildings were particularly close to the trails or river. "All of them mined except for one." Milton pointed to the cabin near the end of a dashed dirt road that branched from another dashed road that stretched from Route 74 to Route 7.

"Why not that one?" Margot asked.

"I figure it was the first one," he said, "and the one that them hunters from Missouri stumbled up on." He looked at me. "I think I got a line on where the next one might be." He pointed to an old house in a U in the river. "That's where the rangers think they'll be."

"Looks like as good a guess as a man could make to me."

"Well, it's the wrong guess." He pointed to the end of the dead-end road. Using a drafting compass, he placed the fixed leg on the end of the road and set the other leg on the farthest barn in which a lab had been found. He drew a circle with its center at the end of the road. The river snaked in and out of the perimeter of the circle. All the marked buildings and one unmarked one fell within the circle. The suspected house didn't.

I looked at him. "You tell the rangers?"

"I just figured it out a little while ago," he said. "I'd almost forgot about that old road."

"Bullshit, Milton."

"Oh, hell," he said. "Don't you wanna make a statement to those assholes?"

"Let's let the law—"

"The hell with the law," he said. "They the ones that got that Lambert boy killed. If they had left people in them houses, wouldn't be no meth labs in them now."

"Milton, that's not very logical."

"You college boys and your goddamn logic."

Looking at him, I saw the face of a man who would defend his homeland and the people in it, no matter what. Everyone was leaving, and only strangers like me or troublemakers like the meth cookers were taking their place. Before I could respond, he went back to his coat and pulled out a Christmas package—a video tape, I could tell—and handed it to me. "Merry Christmas," he said.

"Hell, Milton—"

"It ain't nothing," he said. "Open it."

"It's three weeks till Christmas."

"Hell, Christmas ain't a day. It's spiritual. Open it."

I did, and the movie was *Big Jake.*

"Study on that movie," Milton said. "It shows you can't just run roughshod over somebody's land."

"Thanks, Milton," I said. "But I haven't—"

"Don't worry about it," he said. "As long as you help me out, that's all the present I need."

I glanced at Margot, who'd taken my arm in her hands and was squeezing more tightly as Milton talked. "Well," I said, "count me in."

"You a good man, Frank," he said. "At first I thought you was a little soft, but you shot the hell out of them turkeys. You a good man. I feel like I can trust you."

I shrugged and said, "I'll do my best."

"I know you will."

After he left, Margot was quiet. I decided to watch *Big Jake* and figure out what Milton saw in the movie, or in John Wayne. A few minutes into the movie, after the bad guys had shot up the ranch and taken the boy, Margot said she'd seen enough. I hadn't realized that Margot might be uncomfortable with a scene like that. I started to apologize, but she'd hurried from the room.

I kept watching, an hour or so later hearing Margot filling the tub. Jake formed a posse that included his two sons, both of whom had become modernized: one rode a motorcycle and the other had a fancy automatic pistol. But Jake was a throwback to the old west, and he believed in doing things the old way, which seemed uncivilized to his sons. Sure, Jake got the boy back, but not without him and his sons getting wounded, not without his dog and faithful Indian sidekick getting killed. But Jake showed no remorse about losing his two companions, which bothered me. Then it hit me. Made in the early '70s, when those kinds of clear-cut good-guy/bad-guy movies were dying off, the movie was so tired that even it seemed to admit that the days of making movies like these were over. I wondered what the world would be like when I got old. Would I one day be left behind too?

I didn't know whether Milton wanted that movie to convince me to go out on more patrols with him or not, but it didn't. *Big Jake* was a fantasy—the main characters, though injured, all survive at the end and walk away, one big happy family. I knew from seeing Cody Lambert die that you just don't walk away from death so easily. It eats at you and makes you sick. I had to go out there, but I had to watch out for Milton; I wasn't going to try to be some hero.

I saw Margot's purse on the bar. Thinking of that murder in West Virginia, I stared at the purse for nearly a minute, unzipped it, and pulled out her wallet. There was no driver's license, no identification, no credit cards, no checks—only cash. Hands shaking, I folded the purse back together and snapped it shut. I released the breath I didn't realize I'd been holding, put the wallet back in her purse. I sighed, walked to the bathroom. In the claw-foot tub, she was up to her chin in bubble bath. She looked at me. "Frank, don't go with Milton," she said. "I don't know what I'd do if you didn't come back." She reached for my hand, the warm moistness and softness of hers startling against the calluses, scars, and scabs on mine. "Do you believe me?"

I stared into her eyes, wide with earnestness, and wanted to see the truth. Her face was expectant, waiting, but unrevealing. I pulled my hand away. "Why don't you have a driver's license?"

"You looked in—"

"Where's your driver's license, Margot?" I asked. "And is that even your name?"

Her trembling hands gripped the lip of the tub. "Yes, Frank, it's my name," she said. "I told you I was trying to escape everything."

"How can I be sure?"

"That's why I'm here, Frank."

"In Jessup?"

She watched me for a moment and took my hand again. "With you." She smiled and offered me her hand. "Now help me out."

On Monday, the temperature had dipped into the teens, but the sky was clear and blue, the wind still. I'd beaten Harris to the tourist court by a good half hour, and I was a little late. When he finally showed up and made his way into the cabin, I noticed he'd let his three-day growth pretty much become a beard, which was streaked with white, adding ten or fifteen years to his appearance. He wore tree-bark insulated camouflage, the knees and chest stained from dirt and oil. He reeked of engine fuel. "Moonlighting in a truck stop?" I asked.

"I wish," he said. "My brother-in-law's got an old GMC diesel he's trying to get running. I was helping him yesterday."

"Worst engines on the road."

"Hell, all they did was bore out a regular engine," he said. "With a diesel, you gotta start new. You can't just modify what you've already got, like they tried to do."

We were starting work on number five, the cabin Margot had stayed in. First thing was to tear the ceiling tiles out. We strapped on safety goggles and hard hats, carried crowbars, long-handled pry bars, and claw hammers inside.

As we walked, I glanced at Harris's coveralls and thought about the man Milton and I had found in the woods. "Hey, Harris," I said when we got inside the cabin. "You know Cody Lambert?"

"Yeah, I knew him," he said. "A damn shame."

"You and Cody in Vietnam at the same time?"

"Yeah," he said. "Two different places though. He was a Marine. Survived the Ia Dang Valley and then got it here." He shook his head. "Damn."

"You wouldn't think it'd be so easy to make a landmine."

"Shit, it's easy alright," he said. "You can make a Toe Popper in about five minutes."

"Toe Popper?"

"Yeah," he said. "Ram a piece of bamboo in the ground, put a high-powered rifle shell in it on a nail. You step on it, and it goes off."

"How'd you know it was a Toe Popper?"

"From the description in the paper," he said. "That's what we called them. When you step on it, it goes off. So do toes. Sometimes the slug went clean through a man's foot and got him in the chest or even under the chin." He shook his head again. "Jesus, man, I thought I was away from all that shit when I got back home."

It didn't make sense to me either. Danger could jump up anywhere, and it seemed it was most likely to leap out at you in a place you least expected it.

"But I tell you something," Harris said. "It looks to me like them meth cookers mean business. And I figure if the same thing happened to you and Milton, they wouldn't care no more than they did for Cody Lambert."

He watched me a moment longer and reached his pry bar toward the ceiling. He wedged the forked end into the seam between the panels and pushed it through the tile. "I'm glad as hell you and Milton found your elk killer."

"Well," I said, "he wants to go after those meth cookers now."

He was staring at me, still holding the pry bar against the ceiling. "Go after them?"

I nodded.

The pry bar still impaled in the ceiling, he said, "Dammit, for his sake and yours, you better talk him out of it. You get killed down there, who am I gonna work for? I damn sure don't wanna go back and work in no chicken plant."

"I'll try," I said. But I knew nothing I'd say would change Milton's mind. He watched me a moment longer and said, "Good." He shoved on the bar, ripping the composite material of the ceiling tile. Flecks of brown cardboard-like particles snowed down. Probing beneath the tile, he found a nail and wrested it from the ceiling joist. The tiles sagged. He found another nail, yanked it out, and several tiles fell to the floor. I rammed my pry bar through a seam in the ceiling tiles and began probing for nails. The rest of the tiles, and the roofing nails some jackleg had used to nail them up, came down by lunchtime.

Saturday night, on the trail along the river, Milton and I headed for that house. The air was cold and still and heavy. A few inches of snow had been predicted by early morning.

Margot wasn't happy that I'd come out here. Before I left, she kissed me, her face forced into mine. She held me tighter and longer than I'd expected. As she turned away, I could see her eyes moistening. But she was the real reason I'd decided to go along with Milton: I wanted to see whether she'd still be there when I returned.

From the top of a small ridge, a hundred yards or so away, Milton and I observed the house with binoculars. We were hidden in the trees. Hoping Milton would be wrong about the house, I saw its broken-out windows were dim rectangles of orange, and I clenched my teeth and closed my eyes for several seconds. I opened them, trying to blink away the dread. In the house, light smoke rolled from the tops of the windows then flattened in the sky—confirming the coming snow. We could see the shadows of a couple of men moving inside. Two dirt bikes and a four-wheeler were parked outside.

"They're there, alright," he said.

I looked at Milton, the features of his face barely distinguishable under the brim of his hat and against the backdrop of forest. The river gurgled in the gorge behind him.

"Well," he said, "let's tie the horses up here, go get a closer look."

"Let's just call the rangers, Milton."

"I got something to settle with them bastards," he said and climbed down from Cahill and tied him off. He pulled his shotgun from its case and started toward the old house.

"Dammit, Milton," I said. I dismounted, tied Jack Cutter off, and grabbed my twenty-gauge pump. "Wait up," I whispered as loudly as I could without being heard.

We stopped at the edge of the flat. "Better circle around," Milton whispered. "Might be booby-traps all over. We'll head for the house the same way they come in. They ain't gonna mine their own trail." We stayed in the dense woods, circling the house until we found a trail rutted through the leaves and mud. We left the forest, entering the flat on a belly crawl. About fifty yards away, we paused, downwind now. That bitter stench hung in the air. "Smell that?" he whispered.

I looked at him, not wanting to go any nearer to that house. "Let's crawl back out of here and call the rangers."

He looked through the binoculars and lowered them. "I'm going in," he said. I grabbed his arm. "No, Milton," I said. "Those guys mean business."

He glared at me. "So do I." He yanked his arm away.

"You saw what happened to those bow hunters."

"They didn't know what they was getting into."

"Do you?"

He looked at the house again. "Yep," he said. "But them bastards don't know what's coming." He scowled at me again. "This is our big chance, Frank."

"Milton, those guys would as soon kill you as look at you. They don't care. You do. And if they kill you, this place doesn't have a soul to watch over it."

"Everybody's gotta die sooner or later."

"What about your kids and grandkids?" I said. "You getting killed's a hell of a Christmas present for them."

His face softened.

"And, besides," I said, "I'm too citified to take over for you."

He looked at the house for a few seconds and then at me.

"Let's let the authorities handle it."

"Alright then," he said. "Maybe you're right."

I lolled my head toward the ground, felt the tension release in my back.

We crawled backwards until we made the woods, and we eased back toward the horses. A bright flash of light and a blast came from directly in front of us. Milton staggered back. I saw a figure in the darkness. My right arm stung, but I shot at the figure and dove on the ground. The figure fired again, but this time into the mass of dead leaves, acorn shells, and twigs. The figure staggered and fell. For several moments silence took over.

"What's going on?" someone yelled from the house.

"Milton?" I whispered.

"Goddamn," he cried. "Goddamn. Chest."

"Let's get the hell outta here," another voice said from the house. A motorcycle started up. "Where you going, man?" the first voice called out.

Pumping a shell into the chamber, I could see a figure coming toward us from the house.The guy on the bike headed up the mountain toward the dead-end road.

"Justin?" the figure said, still coming. "I told you not to shoot at nobody else. Justin?"

The voice started registering, but my right arm stung, drawing my attention away from the man. I felt above the elbow, and my coat was moist with blood. I'd caught spray from the shotgun. Climbing to one knee, I aimed my flashlight and gun in the direction of the approaching figure. "Frank, is that you?" he said, and I knew who it was. I closed my eyes for a moment and grimaced, trying not to scream out at him.

"Milton?" he called out.

"Milton's hurt bad, Harris," I said.

"Dammit, Frank," Harris said. "Goddammit." He kicked around in the leaves. Nearly sobbing, he said, "You said you were talking him out of this."

Milton coughed, moaned, worked his legs in the leaves. "Kill him."

"Milton's in trouble, Harris," I said. "We gotta get him out of here."

"I can't do it," he said. "You know I can't."

"Kill the son . . . bitch."

"I'm turning you in, regardless," I said. "Might as well make it look better by helping Milton."

"Take the four-wheeler," he said. He looked in the other figure's direction. "He ain't gonna need it no more. I told him not to be taking the shit."

"Harris, you gotta come with me."

"Frank, watch!" Harris yelled, pointing at the other figure. I saw him from the corner of my eye, struggling to his knees, trying to level his gun at me. I wheeled, fired. My shotgun kicked. The man's body toppled to the ground.

"God," Milton groaned, and then gasped and coughed.

I aimed at Harris now. "Don't move, Harris. Don't make me shoot you too."

"I ain't got no gun on me," he said. "And Frank, I ain't shot nobody. Now I'm gonna get on out of here." He turned back to the house, started walking again.

"Harris," I said, holding the bead on the shotgun barrel on the silhouette of his back. He stopped.

"Here's your chance, Frank."

I put a little pressure on the trigger, closed my left eye, took a breath. Milton coughed again but barely moved. I pulled my finger from the trigger guard, closed both eyes, hung my head, and lowered the gun. I heard him run. He kick-started the bike, took off up the mountain.

I went to the other man, shone the light on him. He lay on his right side. His left shoulder was mangled from my first shot, his left side from my second. A few holes from stray shot freckled his neck and jaw. He wasn't more than eighteen or nineteen, mouth agape, eyes glinting silver. Festering acne covered his face. He was emaciated, like a man being starved.

I nudged him with the toe of my boot. He didn't move. I rolled him onto his back. On a thin chain around his neck was a locket. I started to open it, but I didn't want to see some girlfriend or wife or kid. I was sure he was dead. I wanted to grab my gun by the barrel and sling it through the woods, cursing it as it crashed through the tree limbs, but I was afraid I still might need it.

I hauled Milton out on the four-wheeler, stopping at the rangers' station, where we waited on the state troopers and the ambulances. Two rangers took off on horseback to investigate the scene of the shootings, round up our horses, and guard the dead body. Another ranger questioned us, but Milton was barely hanging on. He lay on a stretcher on a map table. His hands were overlapped across his stomach. I stood over him as he managed to tell the rangers the meth cookers had shot first. I placed my hand on Milton's, which were trembling and cool, crossed over his belly. He grimaced, teeth gritted, eyes closed, and he moaned before growing silent and lying motionless. After Milton's hands no longer rose and fell with his breathing, I removed mine. Trying not to look at him, I called Margot and told her to meet me at the hospital in Harrison, where they'd take Milton and me after I'd answered their questions.

In the hospital emergency room, I had seven pieces of lead shot removed from my arm and it was wrapped with gauze. I'd watched them haul Milton through stainless-steel doors down the hall, shivered when I imagined him lying in the morgue. I thought about that wood stove in Milton's house, how warm it always was in his living room.

After I was patched up, a state trooper came into the examination room to question me. He shook my hand for some reason.

"We have to charge you with homicide," he said. "I'm sorry."

I glanced at him, his face nondescript, chin sharp, eyes hard and green, a flat-top haircut. "Well, I did kill a man," I said.

He nodded. "It doesn't mean you're guilty or anything. Once the investigation's over, you'll likely be cleared. We won't have to hold you. It looks justifiable."

I looked at a skinless rendering of the human body hanging on the wall, the skin, membranes, and muscles cut back a layer at a time, stair-stepped, to reveal bones and organs.

"Amazing what all your skin hides, ain't it?" he said, noting what I was looking at. I nodded.

"You say you're originally from Lincoln?" the trooper asked.

"Yeah," I said. "My folks still live over there."

"I lived in Prairie Grove," he said. "Close to the battlefield. I was stationed over there for a few years. Transferred over here because I thought it would be calmer."

"So did I." He nodded again.

"There were two that got away? You're sure of that?"

"Yeah."

"You recognize them?"

I thought of Harris, his warning to me, that tired look on his face over the last several weeks, how he'd blamed it on his kid. "One of them," I said. "Harris James. He worked for me." The trooper studied me a moment longer, took my statement, and told me I could go.

Margot was sitting in the waiting room. She came to me, took my good arm, and led me to her car. Driving home, she kept glancing at me, but she didn't pry.

I stayed quiet.

At the house, she helped me undress and set me on the edge of the bed. "Harris was one of them," I said.

"The guy who works for you?"

"He saved my life," I said. "Then I let him go."

I felt myself breaking down, something I couldn't control slamming against my insides and my brain. "I was mad enough, I hated him enough, but I couldn't shoot him. Once I saw I was safe, I couldn't shoot anymore."

She ran her fingers through my hair. "It's alright," she said. "I know what you've been through."

"Do you?" I asked. "I mean, my own employee turns out to be a meth cooker. My friend gets shot. I shot a man. You show up here from out of nowhere without a driver's license. I don't know who to trust. Do you really know what I've been through?"

She leaned her head against my shoulder and looked at our reflections in the dresser mirror. "Yes," she said. "I know what it's like to watch someone be killed." She stopped, blinked away tears. "To feel guilty about being alive."

I turned toward her, grabbed her arm, and said, "Are you telling me the truth?" She looked at me. "Are you?"

"Every day," she said, "I wonder why I deserve to be alive. Every day. Every goddamn day."

I glanced at her in the mirror. She ran her fingers across the gauze on my arm. I couldn't feel her touch there. I looked at her in the mirror as if it were she, not her reflection, sitting over there across the dresser from me. For an instant, I panicked, believing that Margot was no more real than that reflection. In a way, I almost wished she weren't real, that meeting her had been a dream; Milton's death might also be a dream. And so would Harris and those meth labs.

I held her with my one good arm, wondering why I shouldn't allow myself to enjoy this person who'd stumbled into my life. I wanted her, and I could think of nothing else to feel. I led her to my bedroom and began undressing her with my one hand. I glided it along the curves of her body, over her ribs and stomach, over her breasts and hardening nipples, over the swell of her hips. I felt as if I were sculpting her, as if I were making her into someone new, someone without a mysterious past. We kissed and she undid my jeans.

In bed she was on top of me, moving against me, her palms pressed into my chest, nails digging into me. The silhouette of her body was the color of a storm in the darkness of the room. For several minutes I ran my hand along her ribs, my fingertips along the recesses between each one. I held her at the taper of her waist and closed my eyes and found her rhythm and pulled her to me. She washed over me and drew me in deeper.

I was a pallbearer for Milton, as were his three sons, who came in from Dallas, Tulsa, and Kansas City, and his two surviving brothers, who both lived in Harrison. All of them told me Milton's death wasn't my fault, but their words seemed to hold up no better than a two-by-four could hold up a bridge. I sweated through the entire service, staring at the poinsettias surrounding the casket. I wished Margot had come, but I understood her not wanting to be around even more death.

When the time came to carry the casket out, I took my place behind Milton's two brothers on the left side of the casket, so I could use my good right arm. I figured I was last in importance among the six pallbearers and decided that hierarchy was ironic. I was the one with Milton when he got killed. As we carried the casket down the aisle, I scanned the congregation for Margot in case she'd slipped in without my seeing her, but I saw only strange faces or faces I'd seen before but couldn't name.

Outside, the other end of the casket was placed on the edge of the opening in the rear of the hearse. Milton's oldest son and oldest brother stepped aside, and the rest of us shoved the casket forward, into the black

Suburban. Four-wheel-drive hearses were necessary around here because of all the old family cemeteries up in the mountains or down in the hollows. The roads to those places were steep, narrow, and usually rutted.

The driver closed and latched the doors. I patted Robbie on the shoulder. We looked at each other a moment without speaking, until Robbie said, "You should've stopped him."

"I tried," I said and removed my hand.

Robbie's face was red and he was shaking, clenching his hands into fists. He looked as though he wanted to fight me, right here. People started gathering around, and I felt conspicuous and glanced away.

"You can't even face me," Robbie said, causing me to refocus on him.

"Robbie," one of his brothers said.

Robbie shot him a look and turned toward me.

I wanted to ask him why he didn't stop Milton, but I knew he was as stubborn as Milton, seemed to have his father's knack for twisting logic. Still, I couldn't look him in the eye. I cleared my throat and said, "I guess we all need to think about how we're accountable."

He started toward me, but his brother took him by the arm. Robbie tried to yank free. His brother held tight with both hands and said, "Let's go, Robbie." He led Robbie through the small crowd toward another long, black Suburban, in which the rest of their family waited to follow the hearse to the cemetery. The entire time, Robbie glared back over his shoulder at me.

At the gravesite, I left my truck and walked to the hearse, where Milton's brothers and sons waited for me. I had to carry my friend one more time, and I dreaded placing that casket on the catafalque, watching the mouth of the grave slowly swallow him. I dreaded having to stare at Robbie one more time once I could no longer shield myself behind the pile of flowers atop the casket between us.

Margot's car was gone when I got home. I sat in the truck for several minutes, staring at the house. I was afraid to go inside, afraid there'd be none of her things, no note, no trace of her anywhere.

Finally, I climbed out and went in. A note was on the bar, folded under the Maker's Mark bottle that we'd drunk from a few nights before. After taking a breath to steady my hands, I unfolded the note and read.

Frank,
I wasn't prepared to meet someone like you. What I wanted wasn't to fall in love. I'm not ready to handle it. Leaving this way is hard, but I have to. I've brought you my tragedy. Remember that I do love you, no matter what you may decide about me. I have to keep moving now, but I know I'll never find myself with someone else again. I will always think of you instead.

Love,
Margot

I read it dozens of times, at first with anger, and then with hurt, longing, and finally regret that I'd left her alone. Suspicion set in. I rushed into my office and called the newspaper in Triple Oaks, West Virginia, asked if they could fax me a picture of Helen Spangler and a copy of the story.

"Do you have information about her?" the voice on the phone said.

"Don't know yet," I said. "Send the fax."

"Can you call back and confirm? This is a big deal here."

"Sure," I said. I gave them my number, hung up, and stood there for a few seconds. I glanced at the fax machine, cold and mechanical. As I waited, I read Margot's note again, trying to find a lie or anything in it to make me want to get back at her. But I couldn't doubt her love, even if I could doubt she was really Margot Bailey. After folding her note and slipping it back into my shirt pocket, I went to the bar, made a drink, and waited. Outside, the dogs started barking and a vehicle pulled in the drive. Thinking it was Margot and wondering how many more of her disappearing/reappearing acts I could take, I ran to the door but saw the Hayes County sheriff's Bronco. Sheriff Duvall climbed out, walked up to the porch. "Mr. Powell," he said, nodding at me.

I let him in.

Inside, he took off his felt cowboy hat and sat on the couch. "Been quite a week for you, ain't it?"

"I've had better." I picked up my drink. "Drink?" I asked.

He winked. "It's a dry county."

I killed the drink.

"I come by to tell you they caught that Harris down in Texas, headed to Mexico. He give up without a fight."

I shook my head, but I was glad Harris hadn't been killed. I wanted the killing to stop, and maybe now it would. My fax machine rang.

Duvall looked in its direction, at me. "You gonna get that?"

I shrugged. "It's just a fax," I said. "Something to do with my business. What about Harris's wife and baby?"

"They was with him. Caught all of them north of Freer—" Duvall paused, chuckled a little. I heard the fax machine printing in my office. "Freer, Texas," he said. "Not for that boy, it ain't."

I wasn't in the mood for irony. "What about his family?"

"They're being drove back up here," he said. "She's liable to lose that baby, less she's got other family to take it."

I looked at him. "Why's that?"

"State ain't gonna take kindly to her endangering a kid like that."

"Maybe Harris made her go."

"Nope," he said. "She said she loved him and would die before she'd let him go alone." He shook his head. "Something how a thing like this keeps dragging more and more people in with it, ain't it?"

The fax ended. I gazed through the front windows, at the ridge tops to the west, a narrow band of lavender sky chasing the sun behind the horizon.

"Harris give any clues as to who was helping him?"

"Maybe." I nodded. "At work he mentioned something about a cousin."

"Round here, that narrows it down to a few dozen people." He was studying me. I made another drink, swallowed hard, and stared outside, trying not to believe Helen Spangler's picture on the flimsy fax paper was rolled up on the tray of my machine. Would she resemble Margot?

"You couldn't recognize anybody other than Harris James for sure?"

I looked at him for a few seconds. "No," I said. "It was dark. I never met the other guy that I know of, so I can't say for sure."

He watched me a moment longer and stood. "Well, I reckon I've taken up enough of your time," he said. "If you can remember anything, anything at all, you let me know."

"I will," I said.

"Sorry you had to go through that," he said. "Old Milton was a good one."

"He was," I said.

Duvall headed for the door, but stopped. "Where's that girlfriend of yours?" he asked.

"She's gone," I said. "She was just passing through."

"Word had it y'all was getting awful tight."

"Just a fling," I said.

He put on his hat and opened the door. "Hope you're getting that booze up in Carroll County," he said, looking at me one last time before leaving.

"I am."

He nodded and walked out. I listened for his truck door to open and shut, for the truck to back out of the drive and head toward Jessup.

When he was out of earshot, I looked at the doorway to my office and pressed my tongue against the roof of my mouth. I tightened my lips to keep them from trembling. Once something started, the rest of me would shake loose. I stood, went to the fax machine. The paper holding a woman's picture was in a roll the size of my thumb, inside out, on the incoming tray. I grabbed the fax and looked at it without unrolling it. I couldn't make out much through the paper, but I couldn't unroll it. Carrying it into the living room, I wadded it up into a ball and placed it on the hearth. I opened the stove door, put a couple of logs on the fire. They flamed up a little. I picked up the wadded fax, held it for several minutes while watching the flames. I tossed the paper wad inside, watched it flare up, its crinkles and edges turning black and curling. Soon the fax was a black ember, all the words and pictures and truth turned to ash.